A SINGLE ROSE

Muriel Barbery

A SINGLE ROSE

*Translated from the French
by Alison Anderson*

Europa
editions

Europa Editions
1 Penn Plaza, Suite 6282
New York, N.Y. 10019
www.europaeditions.com
info@europaeditions.com

Copyright © 2020 by Actes Sud
First publication 2021 by Europa Editions

Translation by Alison Anderson
Original title: *Une rose seule*
Translation copyright © 2021 by Europa Editions

Library of Congress Cataloging in Publication Data is available
ISBN 978-1-60945-677-1

Barbery, Muriel
A Single Rose

Book design by Emanuele Ragnisco
www.mekkanografici.com

Prepress by Grafica Punto Print – Rome

Printed in the USA

to Chevalier, always
to my dead

A SINGLE ROSE

on the roof of hell

1

It is said that in ancient China, during the Northern Song Dynasty, there was a prince who, every year, would have a field of a thousand peonies planted, and in the first days of summer their petals would ripple in the breeze. For six days he would sit on the floor of the wooden pavilion where he was wont to go to admire the moon, drinking a cup of clear tea from time to time, and he would observe the flowers he called his girls. At dawn and at sunset, he would stride through the field.

Early on the seventh day he ordered the massacre.

His servants would lay out the lovely, murdered victims, their stems severed, heads pointing to the east, until only a single flower was left standing on the field, its petals offered to the first monsoon rains. And for the five days that followed, the prince stayed there, drinking dark wine. His entire life was held in those twelve revolutions of the sun; all year long, he thought of nothing else; once they were behind him, he took a vow to die. But the hours he devoted to settling on the chosen one, then delighting in their silent tête-à-tête, contained so many lives in one that the months of mourning were not a sacrifice to him.

What he felt as he gazed at the survivor? A sadness shaped like a sparkling gemstone, shot through with flashes of such pure, intense happiness that his heart faltered.

A Field of a Thousand Peonies

When Rose woke and, looking around her, did not understand where she was, she saw a red peony with sullen petals. Something went through her with a whiff of regret or flown happiness. Ordinarily, this inner agitation scratches at the heart before vanishing like a dream, but on occasion time, transfigured, gives the mind a new transparency. That is what Rose was feeling that morning in her confrontation with this peony, as it revealed its gilded stamens to her from its exquisite vase. For a moment it seemed to her that she could stay for days on end in that bare room, gazing at that flower, feeling more *alive* than she ever had. She observed the tatami mats, the paper panels, the window opening onto branches in the sun, the crumpled peony; finally, she observed herself, as if she were a stranger she had met only the day before.

The evening came back to her in waves—the airport, the long drive through the night, the arrival, the lantern-lit garden, the woman in a kimono kneeling on the raised floor. To the left of the sliding door through which she had come, branches of summer magnolia spilled from a dark vase and caught the light in successive cascades. The shadows on the walls flickered like gleaming water pouring onto the flowers, and all around there was a strange, quivering darkness. Rose could make out walls with sand finishes, flat stones leading to the raised flooring, secret spirits—an entire twilit life suffused with sighs.

The Japanese woman had led her to her room. In the next room, steam for a bath rose from a large basin made of smooth wood. Rose had slid into the scalding water, captivated by the bare simplicity of this damp, silent crypt, its wooded décor, its pure lines. When she stepped out of the bath she wrapped herself in a light cotton kimono, the way one might enter a sanctuary. Similarly, she slipped into the sheets with an inexplicable sentiment of fervor. Then everything faded away.

Now there came a discreet knock, and the door slid open with a soft scraping sound. The woman from the night before came to set a tray by the window, her steps short and precise. She said a few words, took a few gentle, sliding paces backward, then knelt down, bowed, and closed the door again. As she disappeared from view, Rose saw her lowered eyelids flicker, and she was struck by the beauty of her brown kimono belted with an obi embroidered with pink peonies. The memory of her clear voice, each sentence ending on a clipped note, chiming in the air like a gong.

Rose inspected the unfamiliar food, the teapot, the bowl of rice; every movement she made felt like a desecration. Through the bare frame of the window, where a glass pane and its paper screen cover slid open, she could see the etched, trembling leaves of a maple tree and a more expansive vista beyond. There was a river, its banks teeming with wild grasses, and on either side of its pebbled bed were sandy pathways and more maples mingling with cherry trees. In midstream, amid a languid current, stood a gray heron. Fine-weather clouds drifted overhead. Rose was struck by the force of the flowing water. Where am I? she wondered, and although she knew the city was Kyōto, the answer stole away from her like a shadow.

There was another knock on the door. Yes? she called, and

the door opened. The sash of peonies reappeared; this time, the bowing woman said: Rose-san get ready?, and pointed to the bathroom. Rose nodded. What the hell am I doing here? she thought, and although she knew she had come for the reading of her father's will, the answer still eluded her. In the vast empty chapel that was the bath, next to the mirror, a white peony with its petals dipped fleetingly in a carmine ink was drying in the air like a new painting. The morning light pouring through an opening latticed with bamboo cast fireflies against the walls and, for a moment, immersed in the kaleido-scopic play of a stained-glass window, she could have been in a cathedral. She got dressed, went out into the corridor, turned to the right, came back again after reaching a closed door, fol-lowed the meandering of floor and paper. Beyond a turn, the partitions were dark wood in which she could make out slid-ing panels, and after another turn, she found herself in a large room with a live maple tree in the center. Its roots burrowed deep into folds of velvety moss; a fern caressed the trunk, next to a stone lantern; all of it was surrounded by glass paneling, open on the sky. In the shards of a fragmented world, Rose saw the wood floor, the low seats, the lacquered tables, and, to her right, in a large clay vase, an arrangement of branches with unfamiliar leaves, vibrant and light as fairies, but the maple tree punctured the space in which Rose's perceptions were drowning, and she sensed the tree drawing her toward it, her breath responding to its magnetic force, as if it sought to make her body into a shrub with murmuring boughs. After a moment she tore herself from the spell, went over to the other side of the inner garden, where large windows looked out onto the river, and opened a panel that slid soundlessly along its wooden rails. Along the banks with their cherry trees—fluid pulsebeats of space-time—ran morning joggers, and Rose would have liked to slip into their steps that had no past or future, no ties or history; would have liked to be nothing but a moving point in the flow of seasons and mountains passing over cities on its way to the ocean. She looked beyond the river. Her father's house was built at a certain height, above a sandy path visible through the tree branches. On the far shore of the river were the same cherry trees, the same sandy pathway, the same maples and, farther still, overlooking the river, a street, more houses—the city. Finally, at the end of the horizon, a tumble of green hills.

She returned to the sanctuary of the tree. The Japanese woman was waiting for her.

"My name Sayoko," she said to her.

Rose nodded.

"Rose-san go for a stroll?" asked Sayoko.

Then, in accented French, blushing slightly:

"*Promenade?*"

Again those clipped sentence endings, like an echo, those pearly, shell-like eyelids.

Rose hesitated.

"The driver outside," said Sayoko. "Wait for you."

"Oh," said Rose, "all right."

She felt rushed, and behind Sayoko the tree called to her again, strange, seductive.

"I forgot something," she said, and dashed away.

In the bathroom, she found herself facing the white peony, with its blood-lacquered petals and its snowy corolla. Hyoten, she murmured. She stood there for a moment, then, picking up her canvas hat, she left the chapel of silence and water and went to the hall. In the daylight, the magnolia blossoms curved like butterflies—how do they do that, she wondered irritably. Outside the house, the driver from the night before, in a black suit and a white cap, bowed when she appeared. He held the door open for her respectfully, closed it again gently. In the rearview mirror she observed his eyes, thin lines of black ink blinking without revealing the iris, and, oddly, she liked the abyss of that gaze. Before long, he gave her a childlike smile that lit up his waxen face.

They crossed a bridge and, once they were on the other shore, headed toward the hills. She got her first glimpse of the city in a tangle of concrete, electric wires, and neon signs; here and there, the outline of a temple seemed to be adrift on the tide of ugliness. The hills drew nearer, the neighborhood became residential, and finally they drove the length of a canal lined with cherry trees. They got out of the car below a street crowded with shops and wandering tourists. At the top of a hill, they went through a wooden gate—Silver Pavilion, said the driver. His evanescent presence surprised her, as if he had left himself behind to strain toward her, toward her sole satisfaction. She gave him a smile, and he responded with a little nod.

And thus they entered an ancient world of wooden buildings with gray tile roofs. Before them stood strange tall pines set in squares of moss; stone walkways meandered past beds of fine gray sand where parallel lines had been drawn with a rake; a few azaleas had been invited. They went through the gate that led to the main gardens. On the right, next to a pond, with the grace of its curved roofs the old pavilion seemed to be taking flight, and Rose had the unsettling impression that it was breathing, that organic life had taken refuge in these ageless partitions and galleries, these openings of white paper casting their long, milky reflections onto the water. Straight ahead stood a tall mound of sand with a leveled summit; to the left began a vast expanse of the same sand, striped with parallel grooves and curving at the far end into waves on a shore. A view of the ensemble revealed first the mineral flow, then the simulacrum of the mountain with its flattened summit and the pavilion with its winged roofs; farther away, the ponds with their quicksilver water, pine trees pruned as if they were birds prepared for flight, a few more azaleas; everywhere, age-old stones were surrounded by cropped, luminous moss and rooted in the embankments. Finally, the gardens wound their way to an esplanade where the crowd of visitors had massed. Between Rose and the esplanade, maple trees rustled in a cascade of lacy foliage, descending in tiers down the side of the hill.

She was overwhelmed by the beauty, the stone and wood; it all made her feel lethargic, was all so intense; I can't go through this again, she thought, with a mixture of lassitude and terror. But then immediately afterwards: There is something here. Her heart began to pound, she looked around for somewhere to sit. *Like in a land of childhood.* She leaned against the wooden gallery in the main building; an azalea caught her eye; the terror and cheer infused in the mauve petals melted into a new emotion, and she thought she was at the heart of a sanctuary of pure, icy water.

They followed the visitors' path and paused for a moment on the little wooden bridge that spanned the gray water on the way to the maple trees and the upper levels of the garden. All around the ponds there was a parade of other strange, tall pine trees. Rose looked up and took in the branching thunder of the needles against the sky; the dark tree trunks projected the force of the earth into these flashes of plant lightning; she felt herself being sucked into a flow of clouds and moss. The driver's steps were measured; he turned around from time to time to wait for her, showing no impatience, setting off again when she gestured to him. His tranquil pace had a calming effect on Rose, restored to the world a touch of reality which the power of the garden dissolved in the trees. Now the path lined with tall green bamboo led to a stone stairway; she could have reached out to either side to touch the velvety moss where the maples spread their roots. With each step she took, the branches reconstituted a tableau of perfection, and the visual choreography of it touched her heart but also irritated her—and yet her irritation, she realized with surprise, did her good. At last they came out onto the little esplanade; below them were the pavilion, the wooden buildings, the gray tile roofs, the sculpted sand; beyond lay Kyōto and, farther still, other hills. We are east, said the driver and, pointing to the horizon: West mountains.

She assessed the city. Everything about it had to do with the presence of the mountains that, to the east, north, and west, enclosed it at right angles. In reality they were high hills, their shapes conferring an impression of altitude. Green and blue in the morning light, they poured their leafy flat tints toward the city. Ahead of her, beyond a small hill, the city seemed ugly, full of concrete. Rose's gaze returned to the gardens below, and she was struck by their *precision*—the adamantine, obvious fact of them, their purity sharpened with sorrow, the way they were able to resurrect childhood sensations. Like in a dream she used to have, she was struggling in dark, icy water, but in broad daylight, in a profusion of trees, in the blood-specked petals of a white peony. She leaned her elbows on the bamboo railing, stared at the neighboring hill, looked for *something* there. The woman next to her smiled.

"Are you French?" she asked, in an English accent.

Rose turned to her, saw her wrinkled face, gray hair, well-cut jacket.

Not waiting for an answer, the woman continued.

"It's wonderful, isn't it?"

Rose nodded.

"It's the result of centuries of devotion and abnegation."

The Englishwoman laughed at her own words.

"So much pain for a single garden," she said, with a light, frivolous tone.

But she was looking intensely at Rose.

"Well," she said, as Rose still hadn't said anything, "perhaps you prefer English gardens."

She laughed again, absently stroking the railing.

"No," said Rose, "but this place is overwhelming."

She felt like talking about the icy water, hesitated, decided not to.

"I just got here last night," she said in the end.

"Is this your first trip to Kyōto?"

"It's my first trip to Japan."

"Japan is a country where people suffer a great deal, but they don't seem to mind," said the Englishwoman. "In return for this indifference to misfortune, they harvest these gardens where the gods come for tea."

Rose found this irritating.

"I don't think so," she said. "Nothing can make up for suffering."

"Oh, really?" asked the Englishwoman.

"Life is painful," said Rose. "You can't expect any good to come from that."

The Englishwoman looked away, lost in gazing at the pavilion.

"If a person is not prepared to suffer," she said, "they are not prepared to live."

She stood back from the railing and gave Rose a smile.

"Enjoy your stay," she said.

Rose turned to the driver. He was watching the Englishwoman as she vanished below the maple branches, and his expression was one of fear mingled with enmity. Rose started down the hill. When she reached the last of the black stone steps that led to the pond in front of the pavilion she stopped, overcome by the thought that no one, anywhere, was waiting for her. She had come to hear the reading of the will of a father she had not known; her entire life consisted of this succession of ghosts who told her where to go and gave her nothing in return; she was always headed toward emptiness and icy water. She recalled an afternoon in her grandmother's garden—the whiteness of the lilacs, the short grass at the edge of the estate. The Englishwoman's words came back to her and, with them, a surge of rebelliousness. Never again, she said out loud. She gazed at the gray water, the pavilion, the sculpted sand, the maple trees, the garden's large perimeter of childhood and eternity, and she was engulfed by a tide of sadness mingled with flashes of pure happiness.

2

In ancient Japan, in the province of Ise, on the shores of a cove concealed from the ocean, there lived a healer. She knew the virtues of plants, and applied them for those who came to her begging for relief from their afflictions. In spite of this, she herself—as if the gods had made an irreversible, inalterable decision—suffered constantly from the most terrible pain. One day, a prince she had cured thanks to one of her carnation teas said to her: Why don't you use your powers to heal yourself? Because my powers would disappear, she replied, and then how would I heal my fellow man? What care you for the suffering of others if you could live without enduring such pain? asked the prince. She laughed, went out to her garden, cut an armful of blood-red carnations, and handed them to the prince, saying: To whom, then, would I, with a light heart, give my flowers?

An Armful of Blood-Red Carnations

At the age of forty, Rose had not really lived. As a child she had grown up surrounded by magnificent countryside, where she became acquainted with fields and clearings, ephemeral lilacs, blackberries, and bulrushes; and then, in the evening, under cascades of golden clouds and washes of pink, she received the intelligence of the world. As night fell, she read novels, and in this way, through pathways and stories, her soul was crafted. Until one day, as if losing a handkerchief, she lost her predisposition for happiness.

Her young life had been morose. To her the lives of others seemed sparkling and graceful, while her own life, when she tried to think about it, slipped away from her like water through her fingers. Although she had friends, she did not feel drawn to them; lovers drifted through the scenery like shadows, days were spent in the company of indecisive figures. She had not known her father—her mother had left him just before her birth—and of her mother she had known only melancholy and absence. Therefore Rose had been stunned, upon her mother's death, to feel such terrible sorrow. Five years went by, and she referred to herself as an orphan, although she knew that there was a Japanese man somewhere who was her father. She knew his name, knew he was rich. Her mother had occasionally spoken about him, indifferently; her grandmother said nothing. From time to time, she supposed he must think about her; at other times, since she was a redhead with green eyes, she became convinced that Japan was something her mother had made up, that her father didn't exist, that she was born of a void—she did not form any attachments, no one was attached to her, the void was eating away at her life in the same way it had engendered her.

And yet, had Rose been able to see herself as others did, she would have been astonished. They saw her deep hurt as conferring mystery, her suffering sounded like modesty, people thought she led an intense secret life, and as she was pretty, yet austere, she was intimidating and kept desire at a distance. The fact that she was a botanist, on top of it, only increased circumspection; botany was an enigmatic field, and she came across as elegant, a rarity, so in her presence they didn't dare talk about themselves. With the men who passed through her life, her lovemaking was so nonchalant that it might signify either fervor or half-heartedness. What was more, she never felt desire for more than a few days, and she preferred cats to men. She valued flowers and plants but was kept from them by an invisible veil that overshadowed their beauty and deprived them of life—and yet she felt that something, in that bark, those familiar corollas, quivered and sought to befriend her. But the years were passing, and the icy water of her nightmares, a black water in which she was slowly drowning, gradually came to dominate her days. Then her grandmother died; she had no more lovers, stopped seeing friends; icebound, her life was shrinking. One morning a week earlier, a lawyer had contacted her to inform her that her father had died, and she had boarded a flight for Japan. She never questioned her departure; in the void of her life, it mattered as little as all the rest. But her glum compliance with the lawyer's request masked a thirst that Kyōto was now revealing.

Following the driver, she went back out the main gate of the sanctuary and down the street with the little shops. Rose-san hungry? he inquired. She nodded. Simple food, please, she said. He seemed surprised, thought for a moment, then set off again. After the canal, they turned left down to the street below until they reached a little house where a signboard with ideograms stood on the pavement. Ducking under a short curtain, the driver entered through a sliding door, and she followed him into the single room with its smell of grilled fish. In the middle of the room there was a huge ventilation hood above a charcoal grill; to the left, a bar counter with eight places; to the right, behind the oven, shelves sagging with dishes and various utensils above a small countertop; on a low buffet, bottles of sake stood against sand-coated partitions decorated with drawings of cats. All told, the décor of wood and chaos somehow reminded her of the greasy spoons of her childhood.

They sat down at the counter, and the chef appeared, a big man wrapped in a short kimono over matching trousers. A waitress brought them hot towels. Rose-san eat fish or meat? asked the driver. Fish, she replied. He ordered in Japanese. Beer? he then inquired. She nodded. They fell silent. Around them vibrated a presence that their silence revealed, a perfume of innocence wafting over the untidiness of the place, and Rose felt the world pulsing to some ancient rhythm—yes, ancient, she thought, even if that has no meaning. Moreover: we are not alone here. The waitress set down before them a lacquered tray of little containers filled with unfamiliar food, as well as a saucer of sashimi, a bowl with rice, another with clear soup. She said something apologetically. Fish coming soon, translated the driver. The chef put two fish that looked like mackerel, speared with wooden skewers, onto the grill. He was sweating profusely, wiping his face with a white towel, but Rose did not feel disgusted the way she would have in Paris.

She took a sip of ice cold beer and bit into a piece of white sashimi. Ink fish, said the driver. She chewed slowly. The silky mollusk caressed her palate, and, at the same time, images of cats, lakes, and ashes filled her mind. Without knowing why, she felt like laughing until, a moment later, a sharp blade fell— but on what?—and from something that should have been painful, a keen pleasure was born. She took another sip of beer, tasted a red sashimi (fat tuna, he said) that set her senses reeling; so much pleasure born of such bare simplicity, she thought with wonder, as the waitress brought the grilled fish. With her chopsticks, she struggled to pull the flesh apart, con- centrated, eventually opted for a slow, painstaking strategy, and met with success. The taste of the fish was subtle, but she wasn't hungry anymore; she felt unusually calm.

They went back to the house. A man was waiting for her there, a Westerner. He greeted her politely when she came into the room with the maple tree. Next to him Sayoko, her hands folded over her peonies, stood watching her. Rose remained silent. The man stepped toward her. She noticed that he moved in a particular way, traversed the now-liquid space as if navigating between two oceans of reality. She also noticed his light eyes, blue or green, and the line creasing his forehead.
"My name is Paul," he said. "I was your father's assistant."
As she said nothing, he added:
"Maybe you didn't know he was an art dealer?"
She shook her head.
"Of contemporary art."
She looked around her.
"I don't see anything contemporary here," she said.
He smiled.
"There are several sorts of contemporary art."
"Are you French?"
"Belgian. But I've been living here for twenty years."

She guessed he must be roughly her age and wondered what had brought him to Japan at the age of twenty.

"I studied Japanese at the university in Brussels," he said. "When I came to Kyōto, I met Haru, and I started working for him."

"Were you friends?" she asked.

He hesitated.

"He was my mentor, but in the end, yes, you might say we were friends."

Sayoko said something to him, and, nodding his head, he motioned to Rose to sit down at the low table to the left of the maple tree. She took her seat, feeling as if the life inside her was escaping, like the air from a punctured balloon. Sayoko brought some tea in gritty ceramic bowls whose surface was that of ploughed earth. Rose turned hers in her hands, rubbing the irregularities.

"Keisuke Shibata," said Paul.

She looked at him, not understanding.

"The potter. Haru has represented him for over forty years. He's also a poet, a painter, and a calligrapher."

He took a sip of tea.

"How tired are you?" he asked. "I'd like to go over the schedule for the next few days with you; you must tell me how you feel."

"How I feel?" she said. "I don't think fatigue's a major factor."

He looked her in the eyes. She was disconcerted, waited.

"No," he said, "but I'd like to know all the same. We will have plenty of time to talk about the other factors."

"Who says I feel like talking?" she asked, in an aggressive tone she instantly regretted.

He didn't reply.

"What needs to be done?" she asked.

"We have to talk, and on Friday we go to the lawyer's."

He was still looking her straight in the eye, calmly, express-
ing himself without haste. Sayoko reappeared in a door on the
other side of the maple, came to pour some more tea, and went
on standing there, her questioning gaze on Paul, her hands on
her pink peonies.

"There's a peony in the bathroom," said Rose. "It's called
hyoten. They grow it on the island of Daikonshima, in volcanic
soil. Does *hyoten* mean anything in Japanese?"

"It means icy water or, more precisely, the temperature of
icy water, the freezing point," he replied.

Sayoko looked at Rose.

"Volcano ice lady," she said.

"You're a botanist," said Paul.

So? thought Rose, feeling the same irritation she'd felt
when she saw the magnolia blossoms at the entrance.

"He talked about you all the time," he added. "Not one day
went by that he wasn't thinking about you."

The shock of his words came like a slap. He has no right,
she thought. She wanted to say something, but only managed
to nod, not knowing if she was agreeing, or refusing, or if she
even understood what he'd said. He stood up, she did likewise,
robotically.

"I'll let you get some rest, but I'll be back later," he said.
"We'll have dinner in town."

In her room, she collapsed onto the tatami, her arms folded
over her chest. Delicately inserted into a black vase, their heads
bent in a graceful lift, three blood-red carnations cavorted.
They were the Chinese variety, with simple petals and fragile
stems, their carmine color exceptionally intense. The three
corollas, the candor of simple flowers, their perfumed fresh-
ness, all came as a reproach to her; something about the way
they were arranged unsettled her; a wave of exasperation went
through her. She fell asleep. Two quick knocks on the door
woke her with a start.

"Yes?" she said.

"Paul-san waiting for you," came Sayoko's voice.

There was a moment of uncertainty, then she remembered.

"Coming," she said, and thought: Bells, summons, chaperoned outings—this is worse than school.

She wondered how long she had been asleep. A long time, she thought. I'm jet-lagged, I always feel like I'm in the wrong time zone. In the bathroom mirror she saw that the pillow had left deep grooves across her cheek. On impulse she reached for a tube of lipstick, then put it back down. *He talked about you all the time.* She hurled the tube of lipstick as far as it would go, walked back through the bedroom, looked at the carnations, and calmed down.

She found Paul in the room with the maple.

"Shall we go?" he asked, coming toward her.

For the first time, she noticed he had a slight limp, and it was to this condition that she attributed the way he glided through the world like a fish in a river, creating fluidity from something broken. She followed him out to the hall, where the magnolia flowers vied to outperform each other in silent *entrechats*. They walked through the little garden that fronted onto the street. The azaleas unfurled a fireworks display of pink and purple petals. At the foot of the stone lanterns, hostas burst from the same cropped, velvety moss that was visible everywhere; on their right was a row of maple trees, on their left, a white wall where, in the early twilight, the shadows of a bamboo grove flickered.

"Where are we going?" she asked.

"Haru couldn't go out in Kyōto without being recognized. Kitsune was his secret refuge."

As he had that morning, the driver took them to the other bank, and again they went through the streets of concrete and electric wires. Outside the restaurant, to the right of the sliding door, a red lantern looked to Rose like a lighthouse in the dark. Inside, the smoke blurred her gaze. From the rear, from beyond a bar counter crowded with bottles of sake, came effluvia of grilled meat; at the front were four dark wooden tables, the obscurity lit by a few hanging lamps; on the walls painted black there were manga posters, advertising signs, figurines of superheroes; everywhere stood crates of beer, enigmatic bottles, illustrated books; altogether the atmosphere was unusual, wooded, and mischievous. Do all their restaurants look like the attics from our childhoods? she wondered, suddenly aware that she was hungry.

"I pictured Japan as a very sanitized sort of place," she said, "not somewhere you would smell the cooking oil."

"We're not among Protestants," he said, "and I know what I'm talking about. Most of Japan is one happy chaos."

"Not at his place," she said, unable to say *my father's place.*

"Most of Japan," he said again.

The chef stood before them, a young man with glasses and protruding teeth and a headband around his brow. Rose noticed his timid curiosity as Paul exchanged a few friendly words with him; then she thought she heard her father's name, and the young man's expression changed. He took off his glasses and wiped them. There was a moment's silence, and then he said something, looking at her.

"Welcome," Paul translated.

Was that all? she wondered.

"Do you eat meat?" Paul asked.

"What kind of restaurant is this?"

"Yakitori. Grilled meat on skewers."

"That's fine with me," she said.

"Beer or sake?"

"Both."

There was a brief exchange between the two men, and after that she was alone with Paul in a wordless limbo that made her

feel uncomfortable. She gave a start when the chef deposited
two tall glasses of ice cold beer before them. The same thought
she'd had that morning—*we are not alone here*—crossed her
mind again, and then, *What* is *this country where you're never
alone?*

"Haru was from a modest background," Paul said. "This
place reminded him of the yakitori he ate as a child in the
mountains in Takayama."

He raised his glass.

"To your health," he said and, not waiting, took a long sip.

Strangely, she thought of the three red carnations in their
black vase. The chef brought a pile of meat skewers and a bot-
tle of sake to the table. She drank down half her beer, and felt
better.

"The sake is from Takayama," Paul said, pouring her a
glass.

"Takayama? Are you trying to make things all sentimen-
tal?" she asked.

He looked her in the eye in that clear, direct manner of his
that she found disconcerting and took a sip. She noticed the
curve of his brows, his high forehead marked with a vertical
line. The sake was cool and fruity, soft on the palate; the meat
was aromatic. She felt herself getting tipsy. She realized they
had been eating in silence for a while already. Soon the meal
would be finished, and they had hardly spoken. She relaxed,
her initial embarrassment gone. When he began to speak
again, she felt as if she were being torn from a peaceful reverie.

"Haru's greatest regret was that he was unable to give you
anything during his lifetime."

He can't do this, she thought, he cannot go on punching me
in the stomach without warning.

"And why was that?" she asked, exasperated.

He looked at her, startled.

"I assume you know."

I know, yes, I know, she thought angrily.

"Why did he regret it?" she asked again.

He took a sip of beer. His reply came slowly, as he chose his words carefully.

"Because he believed that giving makes one alive."

"He was a Buddhist?" she asked. "And you? Are you a starry-eyed believer, too?"

He laughed.

"I'm an atheist," he replied. "But Haru was a Buddhist, in his way."

"In what way?"

"He was a Buddhist through his love for art. He believed Buddhism was the religion of art par excellence. But he also thought it was the religion of sake."

"Did he drink a lot?"

"Yes, but I never saw him drunk."

He emptied his cup. She gave him a hostile stare.

"I came here because I was asked to come."

"I doubt that very much."

She gave a bitterly ironic laugh.

"What can he give me now?" she asked. "What can absence and death give me? Money? An apology? Lacquered tables?"

He didn't reply. They stopped talking, but as they headed back to the car waiting outside, as the night streamed down upon them like a dark sap, as they went back through the garden with its lanterns and Paul said goodnight by the magnolia branches, she could feel, without knowing what it meant, the flowers at work inside her. She felt that something, in the bark and the corollas, was quivering and trying to befriend her. Exhausted, overwhelmed by the confusion of her thoughts, she fell asleep. During the night she had a dream in which she understood the arrangement of the carnations: they were asking to be taken, they were calling for the gestures of offering. She held out her hand, grasped the stems, pulled them out of the water, let them drip onto the tatami. Then, in the half-light of the same room where she was sleeping, she saw herself holding the three blood-red carnations out to Paul and saying, "To whom, then, would I, with a light heart, give my flowers?"

3

People say that the poet Kobayashi Issa, who, at the time of the European Enlightenment, was living a long, painful life in still-feudal Japan, went one day to Shisen-dō, a Zen Buddhist temple in Kyōto, where he sat for hours on the tatami admiring the garden. A little monk came to him to vaunt the fine nature of the sand, and the beauty of the stones, around which an absolutely pure circle had been raked. Issa remained silent. The little monk eloquently praised the depth of the mineral scene before them; Issa still said nothing. The monk, rather surprised by his silence, extolled the perfection of the circle. And so Issa, pointing with his hand beyond the sand and stones to the splendor of the tall azaleas, said: If you go beyond the circle, you encounter azaleas.

You Encounter Azaleas

Rose awoke to full awareness of the moon's presence. She saw it through the framework of the open window, pearly and solitary, and an image formed in her mind, a landscape of vineyards, and it seemed strange that it had come to haunt her here. It was hot, cicadas were chirring. She stayed there for a moment, eyes open, breathing slowly. The earth was turning, and she was motionless; the winds blew past her, and she stayed where she was. In this silence and darkness she came from nowhere, from no time. She fell asleep again.

On waking, she thought of the dinner the night before, its halo of indefinable presence. She took a shower, got dressed, and went into the maple room, where she found Sayoko wearing a light-colored kimono with an orange obi dotted with gray fireflies. As the Japanese woman gestured to her to sit down, and brought her the same tray as the day before, Rose again admired the diaphanous texture of her eyelids.

"Rose-san sleep well?" Sayoko asked.

Rose nodded.

"Driver say you meet kami yesterday," she added.

"*Kami?*"

"*Kami.* Spirit."

Rose looked at her, puzzled. *I met a spirit yesterday?* Then she remembered the Englishwoman at the Silver Pavilion and the expression on the driver's face as she walked away.

"The British woman?" she asked.

Sayoko looked cross.

"*Kami*," she said again.

Then, with a crease of concern on her brow:

"Bad kami."

She left the room, taking short, stubborn steps. Rose took pleasure in working on her technique for cutting fish with chopsticks—an unfamiliar fish, tender, buttery, which she chewed with a schoolgirl's satisfaction. She decided not to have any rice, poured a cup of green tea, breathed in the fragrance. A wave of emotion brought her to her feet, in need of air, and she went to open the window that looked out onto the river. The force of the water deterred her; she hurriedly returned to the room and found herself right up against the maple tree. Between earth and sky, rooted in its well of light, it absorbed the images created by the cut-grass fragrance of the green tea—tears, wind over fields, sorrow. As the vision faded, she could hear her grandmother's voice in the distance, saying: Please, don't cry in front of the child. And then, as a door slid open somewhere in the house, Rose gave a start. Striding through the air in his fluid, uneven way, Paul was coming toward her, his arms laden with pink peonies.

"Ready for a tour?" he asked Rose, while Sayoko relieved him of the flowers.

At a loss, she nodded. Outside, the driver was waiting. The weather was lovely, a bit cool, and she was surprised by how light she felt. Come on, she thought, it won't be for long, it never is. They went back across the river, but this time they drove up through the hills toward the north. After a moment they turned right up a steep hill and continued through a residential neighborhood of posh houses. The driver stopped outside a wooden entrance.

"Shisen-dō," Paul said. "My favorite at this time of year."

"Is it a temple?" she asked.

He nodded. They climbed a few steps and followed a paved

walkway lined with tall bamboo whose gray stalks and yellow-ish thatch were like a roof of flint and straw. On either side of the path, a strip of light sand streaked with parallel lines was like a mineral stream, and Rose could feel the caress of its tran-quil current, its delicate grain, its ebullient flaxen water. They went up some more steps and found themselves facing the temple. In front of the enclosing wall, a patch of the same sand was home to a single azalea bush. They removed their shoes and went in. After a corridor, a gallery of tatami mats looked out onto the garden. Paul sat down in the middle of the esplanade, and Rose joined him. They were alone.

She saw nothing else. There were plants all around, a breeze through the trees, and rounded bushes, but all her life, its years and hours were contained in the curved lines the rake had traced around a large stone, an azalea, and a clump of hostas, laid on sand so fine that it powdered one's gaze. The world was born of this perfect ellipse; Rose's spirit was dancing with the sand, embracing the grooves, revolving around the stone and the leaves, starting over; there was nothing beyond this endless walk on the ring of days, on the loop of senses; she felt as if she were going mad. She wanted to tear herself away, gave up, sur-rendered to the intoxication of the circuit of stones. She looked farther and saw nothing. The world had gone to hide in this patch of sand and circle.

"We come here mainly in the spring to admire the azaleas," Paul said.

An intuition shot through her like an arrow.

"Is he the one who asked you to take me around like this? Did he come up with the itinerary? The Silver Pavilion, this temple?"

He didn't reply. She looked again at the ellipse, the sand, the lines of its inner worlds. Farther away, the large bushy azal-eas formed a tender green rampart for the dry garden.

"I hadn't noticed the azaleas," she said. "I was looking at the circle."

"In the Zen tradition, the circles are called ensō," he said. "They can be open or closed."

She was astonished by the interest his words aroused in her.

"What do they mean?" she asked.

"Whatever you like," he replied. "Reality matters little here."

"Is that why he wanted you to drag me around from place to place like an unwieldy parcel, to dissolve reality in the circle, drown it in the sand?"

He didn't comment, went on admiring the garden.

"You're a botanist, and you aren't looking at the flowers," he said finally.

There was neither aggression nor judgment in his tone.

"My favorite poem is by Issa," he continued.

He recited the poem in Japanese, then translated.

in this world
we walk on the roof of hell
gazing at flowers

She became aware of a recurrent noise, the same she'd noticed since they arrived at the temple, a sort of sharp clack regularly masking a music of flowing water. Suddenly something changed. The sand was altered, shrank, ran into a familiar hourglass, faded away while the scene expanded, spread into the trees, the birdsong, the murmuring of the breeze. Now she could hear the current of the stream below them, the hollow bamboo swaying against the bed of stones with a sharp clack then going off in the other direction, continuing the flow of water. The maples, the Japanese iris, and, everywhere, the azaleas rooted in the ancient sand—a quiver went through her until everything subsided and she was merely Rose astray in an unfamiliar garden. But somewhere, in a place where reality was of no importance, she planned to look at the flowers. They stood up.

"I suppose you'll be taking me to lunch in a place that he decided on," she said.

"The restaurants weren't his initiative," he answered. "But first I'd like to show you something."

"You have nothing better to do than look after me?" she asked. "Don't you have a family? Don't you work?"

"I have a daughter; she's in good hands," he said. "As for work, that will depend on you."

She considered his response for a moment.

"How old is your daughter?"

"She's ten. Her name is Anna."

She didn't dare inquire about Anna's mother, was put out by the thought that she existed, then banished her from her mind.

Back at the house, in the hall, the morning's pink peonies sketched a complex figure. She followed Paul; they went past her bedroom and right to the end of the corridor. He slid open the door where she'd had to turn around the day before. It was a room with tatami mats and two large picture windows at an angle, one overlooking the river, the other the mountains to the North. Facing east was a low table with a paper lamp, some calligraphy supplies, a few scattered sheets of paper; on the walls facing the windows were large panels of light-colored wood. She looked first at the river, then the mountains with their crests overlapping like folds of cloth, and finally she saw the photographs carefully pinned to the wooden panels.

On one of them was a little redheaded girl in a summer garden. In the background, tall white lilacs sought to hide a wall of dry stone. To the right, one's gaze was drawn to a valley of green and blue hills, a winding stream, a sky of full-bellied clouds. She glanced at the other photos and, after a moment, realized that this was the only one that hadn't been taken on the sly. All the others had been shot through a telephoto lens without her knowledge, taken from various angles, in every season.

"How did he get this?" she asked, going closer to the little redheaded girl.

"Through Paule," he said.

"How?"

"One day, Haru got this photo from her."

"That's it?"

"That's it."

She gazed at the panels. The stolen prints showed her at all ages with her grandmother Paule, with her girlfriends, boyfriends, lovers. Rose knelt on the mat, lowered her head like a penitent. This proof that she was yielding, imploring, revived her anger, and she raised her chin.

"There's not a single photo with my mother," she said.

"No."

"He spied on me my whole life long. And not a single picture with her."

"He wasn't spying on you," said Paul.

She met his clear gaze, felt cornered, exasperated.

"What do you call all this?"

"It's all Maud left for him."

"An entire life without a mother," she said.

She stood up.

"And without a father."

She went on her knees again.

"Did you ever suspect he was watching over you?" asked Paul.

She didn't answer.

"You're angry," he said.

"Wouldn't you be?" she murmured, pointing angrily at the photographs, mortified to hear the trembling in her voice.

There was yet another lost moment between two layers of perception. She looked at the little redheaded girl in the lilac garden; her anger continued to rise, and then, without warning, it transformed. As a child she had known that rough draft of a full life that is referred to as happiness; the emptiness that came later had engulfed her very memory of it. Now that memory was brimming to the surface again, like a bowl overflowing with lovely fruit; she breathed in the fragrance of ripe peaches, she could hear the insects buzzing, she could feel time stretching, languorously; a tune was playing somewhere, at the edge of what is called the heart, or the core, and she let herself drift upon it in a liquid world. Life was woven with threads of silver that wound through the wild grasses in the garden—she followed one of them, shinier, more ardent than the others, and this time it kept extending, continued endlessly into the distance.

"Anger is never solitary," Paul said.

She tore herself from her speechless trance. In a silent crash, the curves of the circle reformed, and she tried in vain to retain the lovely fruit, the way one tries upon waking to hold onto a dream.

"According to Sayoko, the driver said I met a kami at the Silver Pavilion," she said. "A bad kami."

He sat down next to her.

"I didn't meet anyone there. I just exchanged a few words with an Englishwoman, a tourist."

"Sayoko and Kanto have a fairly personal vision of spirits," he said. "I'm not sure their classification is orthodox."

"The Englishwoman told me that if you're not prepared to suffer, you're not prepared to live."

He gave a short laugh, not aimed at her.

"Suffering serves no purpose," she said. "Absolutely none."

"But it exists," he said. "What are we supposed to do about it?"

"Should we accept it just because it exists?"

"Accept it?" he echoed. "I don't think so. But that's the whole issue with the freezing point. Just above freezing, an element is liquid. Just below, it's solid, a prisoner of itself."

"What does that mean? That you have to suffer no matter what?"

"No, I just mean that once you go below freezing, everything congeals together—suffering, pleasure, hope, and despair."

Hyoten, thought Rose. I've had enough of flowers.

"We are a monomaniacal family; my mother was all sadness, and I'm all anger," she said.

"And your grandmother?" he asked.

On leaving the room, she glanced behind her. In the frame of the picture window, the blue mountain ridges melted into a fine-weather mist that rose from the earth and erased their jaggedness and differences in height, varnishing the world in invisible ink, like a powerful, translucent ink wash painting.

In the car she felt like nothing so much as a bad-tempered child. The silence weighed on her, but she was loath to break it; she liked the restaurant Paul had chosen, but refrained from complimenting him on it. They sat at the bar. Everything was smooth, light-colored wood, unadorned, as bare as a hut. Across the room, in an alcove streaming with light, maple branches sprang from an earthenware vase as rough as an oyster shell. Paul placed the order, and two beers arrived instantly. She thought they would eat in silence, but after a few sips he began to speak.

"Haru was born in the mountains near Takayama. The family home was by a waterfall that was frozen for three months out of the year. The family had a sake business in town; his father would go down from the mountain every day on foot. Haru took me there, to stand before a huge stone in midstream, and he told me he'd grown up watching the snow falling or melting on that stone. The boulder had its vocation, along with the trees in the snow, the waterfalls, and the ice."

Ice again, thought Rose.

"At the age of eighteen, he came to Kyōto with no money or training, but very quickly he became acquainted with everyone who had anything to do with *matter*—potters, sculptors, painters, and calligraphers. He made his fortune thanks to their work. He had a natural talent for business. And irresistible charm."

He looked her in the eye. Once again she was irritated, rancorously recalling the ineffable magnolias in the hall.

"However, not a single day of his life was devoted to money. What he wanted was the freedom to honor, in his way, the stone essence of his native stream. And, from the moment you were born, to leave his daughter with a legacy that would provide solace."

"Solace?"

"Solace."

She took a sip of beer. Her hand was trembling. A chef appeared before them and bowed before reaching for some pieces of raw fish in a little refrigerated display case, to the left of the maple bouquet. She had not noticed that they were sitting next to a row of raw flesh, next to octopus tentacles and orange sea urchins; all she saw was the effort she had to make to ward off violence and words—violence and the dead, she thought, overcome with a weariness that was soon undone by the odd excitement this country of trees and stone intermittently aroused in her. The chef placed in front of each of them a square plate of gray and brown ceramic, as rough as a mountain path; on this earthen surface were marinated ginger and fat tuna sushi, which she reached for as if it were a lifesaver, so eager was she to have a body again, to escape her mind, to be nothing but appetite. The combination of tender fish and vinegary rice calmed her. With the relief that came from being in her body once again, she thought that she could understand her father, that she too would be saved by *matter*, by the clay of the world, by a bandage of flesh and rice. Nothing more was said during the meal. Paul took his leave of her by the pink peonies in the hall, saying, I'll come back this evening to take you to dinner; Kanto is at your disposal if you want to go into town this afternoon.

She lay on the tatami mats in her room. I'm walking on the roof of hell without looking at the flowers, she thought, and, at the same time, she saw again the luxuriant azaleas of Shisendō. As she was dozing off, she also saw a circle of extreme loveliness that formed again and again before her inner eye, a circle of deep, lacquered ink floating between dream and reality, tracing an exquisite spiral. Then, as she became enchanted by its endless fluidity, the circle froze and at the same time opened up, a breach where a few clouds roamed.

4

In the Heian era, during the period when Kyōto was the capital of an archipelago lost in solitude, a little girl came one day at dawn to offer rice to the deities at the sanctuary of Fushimi Inari, an hour's walk from the city. As she was approaching the altar she saw, on one side, that during the night pale little irises had bloomed, spotted blue, with orange stamens and a deep purple heart.

A fox sat waiting for her, tucked among the flowers.

After a moment of looking at him, she handed him the rice, but he shook his head sadly until, feeling helpless, she picked an iris and held it up to his snout. He took the flower, chewed on it delicately, then spoke to her in a language she could understand—alas, the memory of his words has since been lost. What is known, however, is that the little girl went on to become the greatest lady of letters in classical Japan and that all her life she wrote about love.

Rose drifted in somnolence for a moment, lulled by an open-circle intoxication, but before long the sensation vanished. Through the window, she saw the flowing river. She took her canvas hat and left the room.

In the large maple room there was no one. She ran her hand over the transparent window, and behind her she heard Sayoko's shuffling little steps. She turned around: again, the rice paper delicacy of those lowered eyelids. They stood for a moment facing each other in a mute comprehension of the foliage; then the spell was broken, and Rose cleared her throat.

"I'm going out for a short stroll," she said.

After a moment, she added:

"A *promenade*."

She crossed the room, but at the last minute she turned and came back.

"Volcano ice lady?" she asked.

Sayoko stared at her and made a gesture that meant, Wait here. She went out, then came back, holding a rectangle of white paper. Rose took it carefully, then turned it over.

"Daughter of father," said Sayoko.

On the yellowed photograph was a boy roughly ten years old, half-turned toward the lens; behind him a cascade of white water between snow-covered rocks; farther still, mountain pines, more icy stones, and an undergrowth of darkness.

"Same look," said Sayoko. "Ice and fire."

Rose resisted the urge to go down on her knees, lower her head, and let the world come down upon the back of her neck. She studied the boy's eyes. The intensity of his gaze made the décor of snow and white water a well of obscurity. She handed the picture back to Sayoko, turned on her heels, and fled. In the garden, she paused. *I am like him.* She went through the bamboo gate, around the house, and onto the sandy path that followed the river. *I have red hair, and I am like him.* She walked for a while, drowning in the power of dark eyes, the power of the torrent. The line that separates water from earth, the line between water and sky: floating lines, sketching a virgin territory with neither wind nor heat, neither ice nor birdsong, an enclave where matter dissolved into the void. A cyclist passed very close to her; she gave a start, realized she was clenching her fists, and came back to earth. The weather was fine, a large heron was lazing in a cove sheltered by rushes, walkers went by. Before long, the embankment grew wider, the sandy path became a strand, the wild grasses in the breeze took on the grace of feathers. Something was turning, slipping. She thought: How many people ever come to know their father through the child he once was? Surprised and troubled, indignant, too, she felt that this was a blessing.

Before her, a dense crowd was crossing a big bridge. She went up a stone ramp and joined the flow of people, borne westward like a twig. The street led to a covered gallery lined with small shops, restaurants, and massage parlors. She had been walking for a long time, she was far away from the house with no money or telephone. She turned to the right and, a bit farther on, entered a stationery shop that smelled of ink and incense; she went over to the blank scrolls hanging against a partition and figured out that they were used for the calligraphy traced on the delicate white square cards that were displayed below the scrolls, their corners held in place by fine cotton hooks. *Every day a new dream of ink.* Next to them, there was incense, too, and incense holders, brushes, refined paper, boxes with motifs of flowers and leaves; she would have liked this world to be her own, would have liked to dissolve into it in a blaze of fragrant wood, a dream of petals and clouds. As she was rubbing her finger lightly over a brush with a crimson handle, she felt someone near her, and she turned to find herself face-to-face with the Englishwoman from the Silver Pavilion.

"Kyōto is not such a big place; you always end up running into people," said the woman.

Holding her hand out:

"I'm Beth. Are you enjoying your stay?"

She was wearing a dress of white silk and, over her shoulders, a long, elegant jacket.

"Wonderfully," answered Rose. "I'm having loads of fun."

"I can see that," said Beth, although Rose could not decide whether she was being ironic.

"Do you live here?" Rose asked.

"More or less," she replied. "And you? What brings you to Japan?"

Rose hesitated and then, astonished, as if hurling herself off a cliff:

"I came for the reading of my father's will."

There was a silence.

"Your father's Japanese?" asked Beth.

Rose nodded.

"You're Haru's daughter?" the Englishwoman asked.

Another silence. Am I Haru's daughter? wondered Rose. I am the daughter of a little boy from the cold mountains.

"You knew him?"

"Yes," Beth said, "I knew him very well."

She glanced over Rose's shoulder.

"You're being followed," she said.

Rose saw Kanto standing by the incense sticks.

"Here," said Beth, handing her a business card. "Call me when you have a moment."

She gave an amused little wave in the direction of the driver and left the shop. Rose went over to Kanto.

"Shall we go back home?" she asked.

He seemed relieved, bowed, motioned to her to follow him. In the gallery, they turned right and before long were out in the open again, heading down a wide avenue, where he hailed a taxi. She was amused by the white lace on the seats, the driver's white gloves and stagey cap. She felt mordant, bitey—*yes, bitey, if that means anything, I want to bite, I want to live to bite.* In the little garden outside the house, the purple azaleas were tastefully wilting, their petals crumpled along delightful creases, their branches set with dying stars. She went through the hall, grazing one of the peonies with her finger. In the maple room she found Paul sitting on the floor, his legs stretched out, ankles crossed, his back against the glass wall. He was reading. He looked up at her when she came in.

"I'm ready for the next rose-colored roller coaster," she said.

"Sarcasm suits you," he replied.

Taken by surprise, she said nothing.

"You were a mischievous child," he added, standing up. "Anyone can see that from the photographs."

She hated what he had just said. To change the subject, she pointed to his book.

"What are you reading?" she asked.

"Poetry."

The ideograms on the cover were like the fine tracings of a reed in the wind; in the gap in a perfect circle of ink, birds and clouds drifted.

"Who by?"

"Kobayashi Issa," he replied.

"Ah, yes, of course, hell and flowers."

"The roof of hell," he said.

It seemed to Rose that they passed the yakitori restaurant from the night before and then, near the Silver Pavilion, turned into the street where she'd had lunch with the driver. The restaurant was indeed located almost directly opposite the childhood greasy spoon, and once again she found herself in a lost land, a reverie of wood, a dream of a life that had fled. On the right, guests were welcomed to an elevated area with paper partitions, tatami mats, and low tables. On the left, a bar counter led to a work area overlooked by shelves sagging with magnificent ceramics. Everything was brown, gray, ocher, and warm; calligraphy and scrolls hung from the sand-finished walls; there were tastefully crinkled paper lamps everywhere; she felt as if she could lose herself in this vanished way of life. They sat down at the bar. Above their heads, spilling from a hanging basket, fringed irises flickered like ghost-lights.

"Iris japonica," she said, looking at the flowers, and then, "What a lovely place."

"Beer?" he asked.

"And sake."

The beers came, ice cold and delicious. A chef arrived behind the counter and began assembling on a narrow plate, crisscrossed with fissures, a mountain chain constructed of unfamiliar vegetables, golden filaments, and bulbs that resembled spring onions, all similarly arranged in little mounds.

"White radish, onions, roots, ginger, local sprouts," Paul said when the chef placed his sculpture before them and a waitress brought bowls filled with a steaming bouillon, a dish of plump white noodles for each of them, and a little bowl with toasted sesame seeds and a wooden spoon.

He pointed to her bowl.

"You add three spoonfuls of sesame seeds, a few vegetables, some udon, you eat, and then you start all over."

The sake arrived, cold and exquisite. Rose sprinkled her sesame seeds into the broth, sensed how they trembled, and felt reinvigorated. She carefully added filaments of ginger, radishes, and various sprouts, then tried to move some noodles to the broth, had to retrieve them clumsily from the wooden countertop, ended up grabbing one of them with her fingers, struggled some more, and stopped, breathless.

"Is this to wear the customer out before they even get started?" she asked.

She looked around, saw that the guests lowered their faces right down to the bowl and noisily slurped up their noodles. She took the plunge and went after a noodle that slid like an eel through her chopsticks and fell back into the broth, splashing the front of her blouse.

"I get it. This is a hazing."

He smiled. She tried something else with the next batch of noodles, sliding them from one bowl to the other, using her chopsticks laterally like tongs.

"I ran into the Englishwoman from the Silver Pavilion in town," she said. "She knew Haru."

He raised his eyebrows, intrigued.

"An older woman, very distinguished?"

"Yes, and she speaks perfect French."

"Beth Scott," he said. "An old friend. She learned of your existence at the funeral, along with half the town."

Rose put her chopsticks down.

"No one knew?"

"Almost no one."

"Who did know?"

"Sayoko and I."

"Who else?"

"No one."

"Not even your wife?"

"My wife is dead," he said.

There was a silence. She wanted to say, *I'm so sorry*, and couldn't.

"Was she Japanese?" she asked.

"She was Belgian, like me."

He put his chopsticks down and took a sip of beer.

"How long ago did she die?" asked Rose.

"Eight years ago."

She thought: his daughter is motherless. In the silence broken only by sips of beer, somewhere in a tenuous, immense place, as invisible as the sky, something changed position. She could sense rain coming, a smell of thirsty soil, grass in the wind. There was yet another shift, a perfume of undergrowth and moss. She began to weep, huge sobs, tears of sparkling pearls. She could feel them forming, flowing, and bursting into the world, adorned with light. She hated herself. She looked down, went on sobbing. Her nose was running. Paul handed her a tissue. She took it, sobbed even harder. He said nothing, calmly finishing his beer. She was grateful to him for that, the flood abated, she regained her self-control.

"I'll take you for a drink," he said, standing up.

The darkness in the car was a balm to Rose. The tears and the sake gave a texture to the city, the patina of a mercury mirror.

"What was the hardest thing?" she asked.

He didn't answer, she thought she must have been indiscreet.

"I'm sorry," she said, "that was indiscreet of me."

He shook his head.

"I'm looking for the right words."

His voice was distant, muffled.

"The absence, initially," he continued. "And then, the obligation, the cross to bear, of finding happiness without Clara."

"Obligation?" echoed Rose. "For your daughter's sake?"

"No," he said, "for mine."

Troubled, she said nothing more.

"You feel as if you no longer speak the same language as other people," he continued. "And you realize it's the language of love."

"I've never spoken it," she said.

"What makes you think that?"

"I don't believe you can give when you've never received, any more than I believe your empty phrases about giving making you alive. Otherwise, what would be the point of giving once you're dead?"

"You're beginning to understand the nature of his sacrifice," he replied.

"This entire farce is pointless," she declared.

The car stopped in a small street in the center of town. They went up an outside staircase to the top floor of a little building of drab concrete and entered a room with large picture windows looking out on the mountains to the East. A bar ran the length of the room, but the decor, with its sand-coated walls and light oak furniture, was overshadowed by the splendor of the mountains, open onto a night of mysteries, the dark poem of the crests. They were alone. As they were taking their seats, a young Japanese woman emerged from a door hidden on the right.

"Sake?" Paul asked Rose.

She nodded.

"I feel like drinking," she said.

"You're not the only one."

She was grateful to him for this unexpected complicity and relaxed. After the first, silent round of sake, he ordered another, and she felt like talking.

"Where is your daughter?"

"On Sadogashima, in the Sea of Japan, with a friend," he replied. "They wander about all day long; she told me today that she forgot her bento in her bicycle basket and a crow attacked it, but she was mostly outraged that no one had thought to make a bento for the crow."

The tenderness of his voice, the images, the story about the crow all seemed annoying to Rose.

"Why did you study Japanese?"

"Because Clara was studying it."

Quite abruptly she felt sober, wanted to say something to reimmerse herself in intoxication, but the door opened and someone came in, yelling. Paul turned around and smiled. The man, an elderly Japanese fellow as wrinkled as a tortoise, was dead drunk. He was wearing a sort of herringbone Borsalino hat, crushed on top. One shirttail was hanging out, and his linen jacket had been through the wars. When he saw Rose and Paul, he raised his arms to the heavens in a sign of cheer and fell flat on the floor. Paul obligingly helped him to his feet, while he let out a flood of joyful words and eventually made his way to the bar.

"Keisuke Shibata, painter, poet, calligrapher, and potter," Paul told Rose.

And lush, thought Rose. Keisuke Shibata bent over and peered up at her from below, blowing his sake breath in her face. Paul gently pulled him back and sat him down on a stool.

"He only speaks Japanese," said Paul.

"Thank God," said Rose.

Keisuke burped conscientiously.

"It shouldn't be too difficult to translate," she said.

"Alas," said Paul, "he's a shameless windbag."

And indeed, the gentleman began to chatter like a magpie, at times addressing Paul, at other times some invisible presence in the room. Rose emptied a few cups of sake. The old man babbled on as he drank. Paul replied in monosyllables and from time to time gave a laugh. Finally, the conversation slowed while the drunkard, his hands flat on the bar, whistled quietly to himself.

"Is he ever sober?" Rose asked.

"Sometimes."

"What's his story?"

"He was born in Hiroshima in 1945. His family was obliterated by the bomb. In 1975, he lost his wife and daughter to an earthquake. In 1985, his eldest son was killed in a diving accident. On March 11, 2011, his other son, a biologist, was on a mission to the Miyagi prefecture on the coast, twenty kilometers from Sendai. He didn't have time to get to higher ground."

With her nail, she scratched at an invisible spot on the bar. Something, somewhere, was threatening. She drank some more sake.

"It was raining the day Nobu's ashes were being interred at the cemetery, and Keisuke collapsed in the mud by his tomb. Haru helped him up and held him close until the end of the ceremony. Someone came over with an umbrella, but he sent them away. They stood there together, motionless, in the rain, and gradually, one after the other, we closed our umbrellas. I remember feeling how heavy, how strong the rain was, then forgetting about it. We'd entered a world of ghosts. We had no more flesh."

He stopped talking, and Rose's feet suddenly felt cold. She tried to cling to the black sky, the kindly mountains. A threat was lurking. She glimpsed shadows, a sudden downpour, foam on the ground. No, she thought forcefully—but rain was falling and she was on her knees, there were no more mountains, no more people, and in this world devoid of flesh, this abyss of closed umbrellas, she was foundering in the mud while all the cemeteries gathered together, and she was merely drifting from one to the next, doomed to a fall, to the mire, to the floods.

"As I looked at Haru and Keisuke, knowing I'd be returning before long to that same cemetery, I thought: We are all prisoners of the furnaces of hell," Paul said.

Next to him, the Japanese poet burped.

"It was raining the day my grandmother died, too," Rose said. "I don't remember any mud, only rain. Everyone says I'm raving, but I could swear the rain was black."

She paused, tried to gather her thoughts, gave up on any effort at coherence.

"Later I read that after the bombs, a black rain fell on Hiroshima and Nagasaki."

She tried again to follow a thread that was eluding her.

"My grandmother loved irises. She loved it when it rained in the garden," she said, thinking, I'm completely drunk.

Suddenly Paule's smiling face appeared before her inner eye. She heard her say, *It's time to divide up the irises*, saw her again in a white dress, leaning gracefully over the flowers, full of silence and love.

Next to them, Keisuke was saying something.

"He's asking who you are," Paul said.

"And who am I?" asked Rose.

There was a brief exchange in Japanese, and Keisuke, mocking, tapped Paul on the shoulder.

"He says you look even more dead than your father," Paul translated.

"Charming," she murmured.

"Completely frozen," he specified.

Keisuke laughed, twittered on as he looked at her.

"He thinks it's good karma, that you have to die a first time in order to be truly born."

"Does he get his pronouncements from fortune cookies?" she asked.

Paul translated, and Keisuke clapped his hands.

"He says you don't know who you are."

Then Keisuke pounded hard on the bar and cried, "Ha!"

"He says it's normal, because you haven't been born yet."

"And when will I be born, according to the Great Boozer in the Sky?"

"I'm not Buddha, you can bloody well figure it out yourself," Paul translated, while Keisuke collapsed onto the bar, farting noisily and beginning to snore, his head on his arms.

She turned to the picture windows. In the starry night, the mountains to the East, sleeping giants under a shroud of ink, spoke a familiar language. Somewhere inside Rose a spring was bubbling, but she knew she could hear and feel because she was drunk, and that the poems and the clear, flowing water would be gone by morning.

"What is it you like about Japan?" she asked.

There was a silence, then Paul said:

"The poetry and the clear-sighted drunkards."

"That's enough to live on?"

As he was getting to his feet, without replying, she imagined that he meant to say: There is only love and, then, death—but he'd held back because she was already dead. Later, during the night, Rose woke up. It was hot. Through the window, through the motionless tree branches, she saw the moon, huge and golden, and she recalled her dream. Sitting in a field of wild irises, looking straight at her, was a fox.

5

During the era of the samurai, on the island of Sado in the Sea of Japan, there lived a hermit who, from morning to night, gazed out at the horizon. He had taken a vow to devote his life to this contemplation, to allow himself to be entirely absorbed by it, to learn the intoxication of being nothing more than a line between the sea and the sky. However, he always placed himself behind a pine tree that prevented him from having an unobstructed view. He was asked why he did this, and he replied: Because there is nothing I fear more than success.

Behind a Pine Tree

In the morning it was raining. The mountains to the East steamed with mist rising into a diaphanous sky; the river was silenced by the downpour. In the pale morning, in the unfathomable, gray, ghost-traveled landscape, sky and water fused and were consumed by the same ending. Rose was tortured by this emptiness yet could not tear herself away from it; in the furnaces of hell, people closed their umbrellas; she had a blind spot regarding her own life, and she wandered through terrain as empty and barren as death. You never leave a front like this, she thought; you cannot fight against something that has no substance. The previous day's carnations had been exchanged for a handful of irises in an eggshell-white vase. The sight of the flowers distracted her from the rain; she had her shower, got dressed, went into the maple room. For a moment it seemed to her that its branches were forming a cross, and stark against a dark sky she saw the crucifixes of places and times whose memory she despised. Then the vision faded, and the tree sparkled. She could no longer see the wayside cross in it, and she liked the fact that it was sprinkled with crystal-clear pearls that stayed there, transparent and trembling. After a moment, she was surprised to see she was alone, and, suddenly, the thought of her father in the cemetery made her go outside. The humidity enveloped her like a tight kimono.

She went back in and found Sayoko wearing a dress and a raincoat, her hair loose, a handbag over her arm.

"Breakfast soon," Sayoko said.

She vanished. After a moment, a phone rang, and after another short while, she reappeared with the usual tray.

"Paul-san meet you at temple," she said. "Today very busy. When Rose-san finish, drive with Kanto-san."

This is like the army, thought Rose petulantly. The day's fish gave her some difficulty, the tea exasperated her. She got up, went to the door where Sayoko had vanished, and opened it.

"Could I get some coffee?" she asked.

In a room with sand-coated walls, a cast iron teapot hung from the ceiling on a chain concealed inside a long bamboo stalk, to dangle above the hearth, which was a simple square hole whence heat rose from embers closely packed on the ashes. A tripod straddled the central area of the hearth, the entire set-up in the middle of a raised area of tatami. All around, the walls were covered with shelving for dishes. Farther along, under the window, there was a sink, then a water heater, soft stone work-tops, and cupboards of light wood. Finally, hanging on the wall was an India ink calligraphy piece that flooded the space with its splashes like comets. The teapot was whistling, the room spoke of fleeting sensations, of a familiar elsewhere where Rose got lost. In her beige cotton dress with a band around her hair, Sayoko seemed younger, slightly vulnerable, and Rose wondered what her story was—was she married, how long had she been working for her father.

"I prepare coffee," Sayoko said.

Rose nodded thanks, was about to close the door again.

"Monsoon is here," added Sayoko. "I give you an umbrella later."

That's all I need, thought Rose, the monsoon.

Then, on impulse, she said: "You take care of people."

Sayoko smiled. On her light, smooth face, a flower bloomed. Terrified, Rose hastily withdrew. I'm losing my marbles, she thought, but she couldn't get away from the vision of the spreading corolla. She pressed her forehead against the cold windowpane; rain was falling, the maple was dripping on the moss; through Sayoko's smile, she drifted off course, in an elsewhere that murmured that she was home.

Rose left the rest of her breakfast, avoided Sayoko's gaze, drank her coffee. At the door to the garden, Sayoko brought her a transparent umbrella. Rose opened it and liked the way she could see the world through the raindrops. In the car, the drive seemed to take a very long time, first west then north, until they reached a vast parking area outside a high enclosure with a huge wooden gate. Paul-san coming soon, said the driver. Rose-san waiting inside or outside? Outside, she said. The sound of rain on her umbrella did her good; for a moment she dreamed of living inside a full, enclosed raindrop, with no elsewhere and no history, no prospects and no desire. She went up to the gate; on the other side, a path of stones threaded its way among temple walls; she turned around and came back. After a few minutes, a taxi stopped next to her, and Paul got out, carrying a transparent umbrella.

"Forgive me," he said, "I had an important sale this morning."

He opened his umbrella; a stray leaf landed on it.

"Have you already had a walk around?"

"No," she said. "Where are we?"

"At Daitoku-ji," he replied, "a complex of Zen Buddhist temples."

"What for you is an important sale?" she asked, as they were walking down the path to where it curved right. "A lot of money?"

"A long-term client," he said.

"What did you sell?"

"A screen. A big screen by one of the most famous living artists in Japan."

"What did it cost?"

"Twenty million yen."

"I can see you're not troubled by cash flow issues."

"You mean you're not, rather," he said.

She stopped in the middle of the path.

"I don't want any money."

He stopped, too.

"You have no idea what you want."

She could detect neither judgment nor reproach in his voice, and wanted to answer, but only made a gesture that meant, I've had enough of this. They went on walking.

"Why do you limp?" she asked.

"A climbing accident."

It had stopped raining. She became aware of the pervasive silence, a *horizontal* silence, pure and incomprehensible—it makes no sense, she thought. And yet the silence hovered over the pathways, and she felt she was slicing through it just below hip level, that it was creating a layer of invisible waves between stone and air. On either side of the passage there were walls, gray roofs, gardens visible through wooden entrances. She tried to keep in mind the fact that she was merely a puppet, traipsing around according to the will of a dead man, but the silence of the place streamed over her, cast her loose among singular thoughts.

They stopped outside the entrance to a temple. On the right, on a wooden sign, she read *Kōtō-in*. Ahead, along a short paved path, ramparts of bamboo and pine yielded to ocher walls; farther along on the left was the arch of a big gate with gray roof tiles. From what was obviously only an antechamber, there came the new feeling of a border, a fragrance from another world.

Rose set off down the path.

The music of the pine trees enveloped her like a liturgy, surrounded her with thorny, twisting branches that tapered into supple needles; a hymn-like atmosphere hovered, the world grew sharper, she felt herself losing all sense of time. It began to rain again, a fine, even rain, so she opened her transparent umbrella—somewhere on the edge of her vision, something stirred. They went through the gate; there was another turn to the right and then, ahead of them, a walkway. Long and narrow, lined with camellia bushes and slopes of bamboo above a silvery moss, surrounded, to the rear, by tall gray bamboo and overhung by an arch of maples, the path led to a gate with a roof of thatch and moss that was planted with irises, languid with the lacework of leaves. In reality it was more than a mere path; this is a journey, thought Rose, a way toward the end or toward the beginning. They took the passageway and, as on the first day, she was overcome with an ancient sorrow that was bathed in bursts of joy, wrested out of nowhere. After two more turns they reached the entrance to the temple. Walking down the corridors to a gallery that overlooked a wide perimeter of moss, Rose felt at home. There was more bamboo here, more maple, a stone lantern, but above all a manner of freedom, an open arrangement where thatch and trees seemed to sport in the wind. She breathed lightly, overcome with a sensation of *possibility*, swept away toward a delightful vanishing point—freer, imperfect, and alive.

Bowls of frothy green tea were brought; she peered at the tea, reticently.

"Matcha," said Paul, looking at her.

Then, as she was hesitating:

"Go on, life is made for trying things."

Reluctantly, she lifted the bowl to her lips. In the taste of greenery, the onslaught of leaves and grass, of duckweed and watercress, she read the land of rice and mountains to which she had been brought—a land where salt and sugar had been removed from everything to preserve a taste that had no spine, a taste of nothing, a smooth, pale concentrate of the forest from a time before humans lived there. The taste of nothing, the taste of everything, she thought. This country's driving me crazy.

"This country's driving me crazy," she said.

He laughed, and she didn't know whether it meant approval or derision. She tried to define the drifting sensation she felt.

"There's something to do with childhood," she added.

"You don't like that?" he asked.

"I don't see that there's anything good about childhood."

"But it's not something you can just get rid of."

"So that's your constant argument, that it's there, so we just have to live with it?" she said.

"It doesn't mean resignation. I'm just trying to understand what is defeat and what is wisdom."

"Defeat?" she asked. "If there's defeat, where's the victory?"

He looked around him.

"Life is transformation. These gardens are melancholy transformed into joy, pain transmuted into pleasure. What you see here is hell turned to beauty."

"No one lives in a Zen garden," she retorted.

They left the temple by the path of wonders and found themselves once more in the antechamber of pine trees. She remembered the gardens at the Silver Pavilion, pruned to precision with the sharpness of a sword, and those they had just visited, supple and carefree, at Kōtō-in—then she recalled that she had walked through those first gardens, too, as if they were a land of childhood, and understood that each garden carried its own share of innocence and of the blade, that they walked there together on the roof of hell admiring the trees, that this pendulum swing between the candor of happiness and the cruelty of desire was life itself. She stayed for a moment gazing at the pine trees. It began to rain harder, and they opened their umbrellas.

Later, the driver dropped them off at the entrance to the bridge she had walked across the day before. It had stopped raining, and Paul leaned for a moment on the railing to look at the mountains to the North. Navy blue against the dark gray of the sky, they shot powerful salvos of vapor into the invisible vault. A dense crowd went past behind them—young people out on the town, tourists, ordinary men and women going about their business in a life that Rose found inaccessible and cruel. A maiko went by them, her air grave, her expression serious.

"The Sanjo bridge always grinds my heart," Paul said, following the maiko with his gaze.

Rose observed the woman's white neck, imagined a life of secrets, of weeping in the night.

"Not my words, Keisuke's," he added.

the Sanjo bridge always grinds my heart
like a tender grain of rice and changes it
into flour on the neck of a maiko

She followed him to the same shopping street she'd gone into, but this time they turned left to a restaurant with a long counter of light wood. Paul greeted the waitress and continued to a room at the back containing a single large table. The light enfolded them in a silky breath of air; Rose saw the light and felt the breath as they touched her gaze and skin at the same time. During the lunch, orchestrated as a succession of strange, fiddly little dishes, they did not speak. At the end, Paul ordered coffee, and she felt like talking.

"That tea this morning had almost no taste, and yet it tasted of everything," she ventured.

"That's a good definition of Japan," he said.

She pursued her thought.

"My grandmother said that everything seemed to crush my mother, that she viewed life as a single block of granite, one overwhelming mass."

"There is a property belonging to the Imperial estate, to the west of the city, known as the Villa Katsura."

He fell silent.

"And?" she said.

He didn't answer. He was thinking.

"At the entrance, the view onto the garden and the ponds is blocked by a pine tree in such a way that you can't take it all in at once," he continued. "Maybe life is no more than a picture you can see from behind a tree. We are offered life as a whole, but we can only see it through a succession of viewpoints. Depression makes you blind to perspectives. Life as a whole crushes you."

She banished from her mind the images that were stealing in, and focused on the trees of Kōtō-in, on the setting of moss and foliage where a lantern had dropped anchor; she lost herself in the branches, attentive to their calligraphy, their unspoken text. They are prisoners of the earth, she thought, and yet they are the possibility of life, pruned to speak of roots and of flight, of great weight and lightness, of the power of our acts, despite our prisons. Then her gloomy mood got the upper hand again.

"Life always ends up crushing us," she said. "What's the point of trying, since we're in prison?"

"Where's the risk?" he asked. "The mere fact of being alive means that all the risks have already been taken."

Alone again in her father's house, she wandered idly between her room and the maple room. The doors along the corridor were inviting, but whenever she held out her hand to

one of them, she was seized by a feeling of sacrilege. The recollection of the maiko's grave expression made her go and sit
opposite the tree in its glass cage. Her thoughts drifted; time
went by with glacial immobility. I'm afraid, she thought suddenly, and an image came out of nowhere. When? she wondered, seeing again the fresh corolla placed next to a botanical
map with hazy edges. The hawthorn petals were vibrating gently, she saw herself taking a few notes; the décor vanished;
somewhere inside her, the flower was fluttering. *I was studying,
I was learning the trade.* She tried to recall the moment, then
was struck by the pointlessness of her endeavor and, with it, of
any endeavor. And so the image yielded to yet another, and
behind the torn scrim of memory, she received her mother's
smiling face. In the tremulousness of memory, her mother
seemed more real, more true than in the past, and the irony of
such an incarnation elicited a harsh laugh from Rose. In thirty-
five years, how many smiles had there been? she thought, bitterly, and everything came back all at once—Paule's kitchen,
the flower and the map on the table, Maud standing before
her, luminous, all shadows flown, smiling and saying, Is that a
hawthorn? How old was I? thought Rose. Twenty? A hundred,
for sure. And then: What is the hardest kind of mourning?
When you mourn for what you've lost, or for what you've
never had? Then, suddenly, she thought about the pine tree at
the Villa Katsura that prevented you from seeing all of life, and
again she told herself: I'm not afraid of failing, I'm afraid of
succeeding.

6

There is in Kyōto an ordinary temple that has none of the beauty of the city's great jewels, but it is beloved for its plot of two thousand plum trees, and the entire city goes for walks there during the final days of February. And yet Issa, the magnificent poet, only went there when the wood of the trees was still black and barren, devoid of the flowers that would later fill the surroundings with fragrance. The moment the first corolla appeared, Issa left the plot behind, while his peers came to admire the miracle of petals cast along the wintery branches. If, now and again, someone showed concern regarding this inclination that robbed him of the loveliest show of blooms all year, he would laugh and say: I have waited a long time in deprivation; now the plum blossom is inside me.

The Plum Blossom Is Inside Me

Maud, Rose's mother, had grown up in melancholy, and no matter what she did later in life, she held fast to it, with admirable perseverance. Time washed life with rain, brought sunshine, the moon glowed, and Maud remained in darkness. What is more, she inhabited her sorrow the way a fox inhabits its den; when she emerged into the woods, it was only to retreat, unchanged, into her burrow; despite Paule's best efforts, she washed up against hard stone cliffs. After a certain amount of time had gone by, Paule gave up, brokenhearted and tired of trying. The years passed, heavy with cloud cover; Maud worked, traveled, came home, unchangeable in her sorrowful castle. And so when she returned from Kyōto bearing the child of a man she had immediately abandoned, Paule was overwhelmed. She wanted Maud to promise that the infant would know her father, and she came up against a rage the likes of which she'd never seen, the only ripple her daughter had ever made on the still sea of her melancholy.

Rose was born, and owed her name to Paule, who loved flowers and wanted her granddaughter to spend time with them. Before long, Maud stopped working and spent her days in the living room, facing the conservatory, ignoring the lilacs. From time to time she wept but, as with everything, with little conviction—so Paule would take Rose out to the garden, not imagining she might actually be able to protect her. For ten years, however, Paule held her breath and wanted to believe in the miracle: in fact, Rose was a charming child, who read, was curious, laughed all day long. Then, one evening, after a decade during which Rose had not heard her mother's tears, they suddenly caused her, too, to founder. To a certain Haru Ueno, whose name and address were on a letter sent to Maud, Paule forwarded the last photograph she had of Rose from before it all changed so suddenly. On the back she simply signed *Paule*, and never found out whether he'd received the letter, or been tempted to reply, to overstep the bounds; for a long time this haunted her.

In his letter to Maud, Haru Ueno wrote only: *I will respect your wish, I will not try to see my daughter, don't hurt yourself.* One day, when Rose was celebrating her twentieth birthday, Paule realized she must have read it. When? she asked, but she knew the answer. You said nothing for ten years? she added. Rose nodded and they spoke no more of it for another decade and a half. That year, one evening in June, Maud went to the river with her pockets full of stones and drowned in magnificent silence, after admiring the trees in the mirror of calm water.

"All that for this," Rose said angrily.

"Now you can meet your father," murmured Paule.

"I could have met him sooner," answered Rose. "The letter wasn't for me."

Then the silence came back to deafen their lives. Two years later, it was Paule's turn to die. That same evening, Rose made love with her lover of the moment with such cruel indifference that she did not feel him withdraw from her, did not hear him leave the room, did not remember, the next day, having had him in her bed, in her body, in her now-bloodless life. A few months went by where she did not recognize herself anymore. A sort of relief came from defeat, and she stopped trying to be happy; her desire to be happy was already so tenuous, and had been thus for so long, that it gave way, indolently. Three years drifted by in this shapeless lethargy. Finally, she took a plane to Kyōto.

She woke up to a sentiment of rain and misfortune. The sound of the falling water made the world evanescent, distant. She went to the maple room, found it bathed in a strange clarity. A fragment of joy burst from this darkness shimmering with rain.

Sayoko emerged from the kitchen.

"Paul-san coming," she said. "Rose-san want tea?"

"Coffee, please," she replied.

She would have liked to keep her there, ask her who she was, why she spoke English. The Japanese woman sensed her hesitation, stood there for a moment, but as Rose didn't say anything, she went away. She came back with an irregularly shaped red cup, as delicate as a poppy, and looked at Rose as she drank.

"Rose-san beautiful," she said.

Surprised, Rose set her cup down.

"Japanese people always find Western people beautiful," she said.

Sayoko laughed.

"Not always. Too fat."

They heard the door in the entrance slide open.

"I remember your mother," said Sayoko. "Very sad."

Finally, when Paul entered the room, she slipped away.

"Where are we going today?" asked Rose.

"Shinnyo-dō."

"Let me guess: a Buddhist temple?"

"A Buddhist temple."

In the car, she felt as if her life were following the vanishing lines of the gray streets.

"Will it rain for long?" she asked.

"For a while, but you'll miss the cool monsoon air when the summer heat begins."

"Not a great climate you've got here."

"You get used to it."

"Japan, the country where they suffer a great deal and don't seem to mind," she recalled.

He seemed surprised.

"That's what your friend Beth Scott told me the first day."

"Beth has a romantic vision of Japan," said Paul. "She's one of those people who live in a Zen garden."

The car stopped next to a stone walkway that led to a red gate then climbed up to a temple and a pagoda of dark wood. It had stopped raining, they did not take their umbrellas, and they stepped out of the car into a fragrance of damp earth and unfamiliar flowers. Rose started up the walkway, then turned around, sensing a presence. There was no one. Farther along, the great courtyard of the temple was deserted, but the sensation grew stronger. *We are not alone here.* Because of these silent, invisible beings she knew nothing about, whose presence draped the world in a new brilliance, she felt as if she were floating aimlessly on the thickness of time. She looked around her at the maple trees, the wooden pagoda; she looked at the great dark temple perched on its solitary hill—without tourists, without visitors. Where did it come from, this feeling that they were among company, that spirits surrounded them, leading them into secret hideaways? At the same time, she perceived something *mischievous*; nothing made sense, everything was saturated with sense; what is this place, she wondered.

"What is this place?" she said out loud.

"A temple where Haru used to come walking every week."

"It's inhabited," she said, aware of the nonsensical nature of what she had just said.

"It's a place of the spirit."

She was surprised by her own exasperated response.

"Don't you ever get tired of being so starchy and sententious?"

For the first time since she'd met him he seemed annoyed.

"You leave me no room for anything else."

"You're a dead man's flunky; that's what makes you so uptight and insipid," she continued.

"I'm the executor of a man I admired, and in keeping with his request, I've been dragging his pain-in-the-ass daughter around from one temple to the next. Is that what you want? You want me to join your depressive-aggressive little game?"

Leaving her there, he walked off, going to the right around the temple and disappearing from view. She stood there motionless for a moment, furious at herself for being so stupid, for having hurt him, relieved, too, that in the end he was simply ordinary. Great sage, my ass, she said out loud, and laughed. Knowing that she would apologize did her good. She was charmed by the mischief of the spirits of the place. What are you? she said, again, out loud. *Kami*? Ghosts? She followed the path Paul had taken, found herself behind the temple, beneath an incurably graceful archway of maples, then turned right alongside high walls. Ahead of her in the distance she saw tombs—a cemetery, she thought, that's what was missing. She held her breath as she walked among the graves, the lanterns, the heavenly bamboo. There were stones shaped like faceless characters and long wooden stems clicking in the wind; featuring close writing, the stems surrounded the graves, simple marble plinths where a narrower stele stood; some of them had been eroded by the years, invaded by lichen. On either side, seasonal flowers had been placed in tall vases of the same marble. Everywhere, the moss rippled, glinting tender, blue, everywhere the lanterns' winged hats cast an impish note into the air. In the silence of the dead, life was drawn out, and sparkled at the same time. Tall evergreen trees rustled in the wind; something else, too, rustled in a glittering of unknown magic, in the craftsmanship of the tombs and temples, the clacking stems, the crows' cries. The birds circled slowly above the roofs, and Rose liked their dissonant call—close to breaking, she thought, and yet so calm. Then: what a place. She continued on her way and saw that she was now at the top of a hill. To the right stretched the city in its basin. At the end of the path, sitting on the top step of a long stairway that led down to other tombs and other temples, Paul was waiting for her, gazing out at Kyōto. She sat down next to him.

"I'm sorry," she said.

"You're not sorry," he fired back. "You are a professional pain in the ass."

He laughed.

"That's absolutely fine by me; I'm tired of being understanding," he added.

On the far side of the city, slightly dimmed in the rising twilight, the mountains to the West glistened faintly. From the clouds a dark, electric light fell; varnished with showers, the temple roofs gleamed like watered silk. At day's end, Rose was no longer shocked by the ugliness of the modern city. There were no skyscrapers to be seen, the stark outlines of concrete had been smudged into a drab whole. Paul stood up, and she followed him down the steps. The wind had dropped, it was warm and humid, she felt herself descending past a row of spirits, past years that had fled, leaving no memory behind. Near the bottom they turned left onto a short path that ended behind a temple. Paul stopped next to a tomb.

"This is Kurodani," he said, "with Clara's ashes, and Keisuke's son Nobu's, and Haru's."

She gazed at her father's tomb.

"What am I supposed to feel?" she asked.

"I have no idea," he replied.

She looked up at the top of the stairway.

"This place is extraordinary, but I don't know why," she said.

Something inside her fluttered like a dragonfly. The ineffable presences, the heavenly bamboo, the gaiety of the stones held a singular service, and for a moment she felt dizzy. She was startled by a gust of wind lost amid the calm of evening, and she shivered. The tomb did not speak to her but seemed to cast invisible fishhooks to lodge in her flesh, and although it was subtle, she detected a mutation in the flatness of the moment—nothing spectacular, she thought, unless I'm growing gills. Abruptly, she went to her knees and, with the flat of her hand, touched the damp earth by the grave. *Matter.* Here lies my father, she thought. She stood up. Everything was identical; everything had *mutated.* She felt drained, exhausted. She looked at Paul. He was weeping.

There was a brief rain shower as they left and headed down a silent street to where Kanto was waiting for them by the car, in the dark. Rose was becoming intoxicated by an awareness of the earth—space had dilated, the air was exhaling a perfume of violets. Paul said nothing, but between them there was a new intimacy—it's better than sex, she thought. In the car, she took his hand, briefly. He squeezed it, did not look at her.

At the restaurant, a sort of bar where people drank and nibbled on little fried meat skewers, they were silent for a moment. The chiaroscuro of the place gave objects and faces a warm, slightly moving iridescence. In a lighted alcove, luminous specks danced on an arrangement of bare branches. The sake deepened their intimacy, Rose felt light, gently tipsy without being drunk.

"No flowers," she said, pointing to the vase in the alcove.

"Plum tree branches," he said. "The Japanese like them even better than cherry trees."

"But it's not the season."

"It might be a tribute to Issa. He only walked among the plum trees before they bloomed, and when they asked him why, he would say, The flower is inside me."

She took a sip of the ice cold, almost white sake.

"The cemetery wasn't on the agenda today," she said.

He put his cup down, looked at her pensively.

"It was not one of Haru's requests," she added.

"I don't go to Kurodani often," he said eventually. "When I'm there, I'm not thinking about my dead, I'm thinking about their funerals."

My dead, she repeated inwardly. Do I have anyone I can refer to as *my dead*?

"The hardest thing, it turns out, is not trying to be happy without the person you loved," he continued. "It's changing, no longer being who you were with that person."

"Do you feel as if you're betraying your wife?" Rose asked.

"I feel like I'm betraying my own self," he replied.

They left the restaurant as the sky cleared briefly. In the open bowl of clouds, an enormous moon was shining, faintly reddish.

"We're not that far from the house," he said. "Would you like to walk?"

He sent Kanto home, and they walked along the river, on the moonlit banks, brushing past tall grasses that bent and stretched like ballerinas. A few people out strolling went by, their faces blanched by the moon; it was chilly, Paul gave her his jacket. He was lost in thought; she continued walking, full of exaltation. The cemetery was speaking to her, her father's tomb was calling to her, inside her she felt the workings of death, without it being a burden; now these workings took the form of a circle dance where cheerful spirits stepped in, uncertain and familiar silhouettes; the memory of the deserted temple was veiled in a silver film, in an afterwards that gave the invisible presences their true shape. Devils, she murmured, oh merry devils, come to me the way you used to—and she smiled at this sudden recollection of long-ago fairy tales. They came to the house, and by the sliding door Paul took leave of her. She would have liked to keep him there, he took a step back, smiled at her. The moon disappeared behind a cloud, she couldn't see him anymore, she heard him close the gate and walk away, his calm, uneven gait.

During the night, she dreamed she was walking with her father through a field of plum trees near a dark wooden temple. Walking behind them were the devils of her childhood fairy tales. Stopping by a flower of extreme beauty, with petals sparkling like diamonds, stamens like lines of clear ink, Haru held out his hand to her and said: You will risk suffering, giving, the unknown, love, failure, and great change. And so, just as the plum blossom is in me, my entire life will pass into you.

gazing at flowers

7

During the era of the great shoguns, toward the end of medieval times, there came a winter so harsh that the rivers of the archipelago froze over, and animals could no longer drink from the streams. One morning in February, on leaving his house, a little boy came upon a ferret. Are you thirsty? he asked it after a moment of tender observation passed between them. The ferret inclined its snout, and the boy led it over to a bouquet of violets that had broken through the ice during the night. There he said, Drink from the flowers, and the ferret licked the tiny purple scapes avidly. What do we know about this little boy today? Not much, to be honest— but we do know that he became one of the founders of the Way of Tea, and that one day he composed a poem that spoke of violets in the ice.

R ose awoke and looked out the window. The slopes were
bathed in thick mist that rose in successive inhalations
toward a transparent sky. It had stopped raining; the
river gave off a heavy scent of earth. Paul, she thought, then:
Everything eludes me.

In the maple room, Sayoko brought her breakfast, wearing
a black kimono decorated with wisteria blossoms.

"Paul-san in Tokyo today," she said. "Rose-san go to temple
with Kanto-san."

"In Tōkyō?" she asked. "This was planned?"

"Very important client," said Sayoko.

"When will he be back?"

"Day after tomorrow."

Left by the wayside, thought Rose. The cawing of a crow
outside exasperated her; impatient, she stood up, went to
her bedroom, and came back with Beth Scott's business
card.

"Can you call her?" she asked.

The crystal of Sayoko's clipped sentences only increased her
frustration; she reached brusquely for the receiver.

"Do you have some time today?" she asked the Englishwoman.

"This afternoon," Beth replied. "I'll explain to Sayoko where
to meet."

Sayoko took the telephone, listened, and hung up, an

imperceptible pout of disapproval on her face. She doesn't like her, thought Rose, with spiteful satisfaction.

"I won't go to the temple," she said.

"Yes, you go," said Sayoko placidly.

Rose felt like saying *go to hell*, thought better of it, went out, crossed the garden, where the rain-blemished azaleas looked wretched to her, then got in the car, slamming the door. During the drive toward the mountains to the East she looked only at her hands. When Kanto stopped and said, This is Nanzen-ji, she got out, slamming the door again, took a few enraged steps, stumbled. Behind her, Kanto added, Temple there. She turned around and saw that he was pointing to the very end of a tree-lined path.

It was an extraordinary place—temples everywhere, trees, moss, tall gates with curved wings. She walked to a huge gate with two roof levels, one story of paper partitions, and a cap of gray tiles. Through it, maple branches were visible, and, in the distance, in front of a temple, was a huge incense holder diffusing pale curls of smoke. It was windy, and you could hear the clicking of the invisible bamboo; the air smelled of rain. She climbed the steps that led to a gate with two large rectangular openings, supported by gigantic pillars. She went through it and felt as if she had passed through an invisible screen, then strode up the path to the bronze basin. The incense made the world thick; walking through the layers of scent, she could feel their seal leaving an imprint. Turning right, she reached the main walkway and followed it to the entrance of Nanzen-ji. Kanto showed up behind her, paid for her entrance, handed her a piece of paper, and went off again. She was surprised by the whiteness of the outside walls, as well as the semidarkness of the wooden inner galleries. Through this gloomy prologue, as she reentered the light something gripped her by the throat. *For the first time I can see.* She sat on the floor, stayed there gazing at the rectangle of sand and foliage. All around ran inner galleries, then walls topped by gray tiles. Along the front, gray sand had been raked into parallel lines, both straight and curved. In the back, in front of the wall, four trees were like music notes on a score, caressed by a movement of moss, ancient stones, and a few azalea shrubs. It was the most sober, most oddly *outdated* garden she had ever seen, as if it had returned from a passage through geological eons, and yet, everything about it was alive—the stillness in motion, she thought, limpid and vibrant, the absolute presence of things, the final lesson of the world. How many centuries to attain this absolute present? She looked up and saw sand, moss, trees, walls, and tiles, superimposed; beyond them, the trees held tightly to the hillside, set out like sculptures, launched at last toward the ink of the sky; she saw the living spirit of architecture, its changing, perfect nature—she said it out loud: perfect. She thought of Paul and felt a pang in her heart. After a moment, she went to walk along the other galleries, found the adjacent gardens ordinary, came back to the initial tableau, and strayed into it again. Leaving was an exquisite, wrenching moment. I will come back, she said, again out loud.

She found Kanto out in the little parking lot; she felt new, elemental. He locked the car, pointed to the street below and said, Going to eat now. Eat what? she asked. Tofu, he replied. She followed him past little temples fronted by tiny gardens with calligraphic trees. Farther along, on the left, they went through a gate, took an alleyway lined on one side with maples and moss and on the other with a large hall of tatami mats visible through slightly blurry windowpanes. They were asked to remove their shoes and then invited to sit on cushions at a table with a little stove. Only one menu, said Kanto. She bit into a cube of tofu brushed with green sauce, was surprised by the flavor of soy sauce and an unfamiliar herb, and laughed for no reason; Kanto remained impassive; again they were served a toasted tea when she would have preferred a beer. Meet Scott-san now, he said. She followed him out to the car, watched the streets rush by without seeing them, gave a start when Kanto came to open her door. Scott-san inside, he said, pointing to an entrance hidden by short curtains.

Nanzen-ji was still having an effect on her, and she felt as if she were wrapped in a veil of mineral substance, where something was drifting off course, something was turning liquid. She entered the tea house through a glass door hidden behind four cloth hangings printed with ideograms. It was an old building with dark walls and a roof and awning covered with gray tiles; inside was a dream of wood, worn shelves holding ancient jars of tea sealed with orange cords ending in long tassels; a press of young women in light blouses, green aprons, and white kerchiefs resting on their hair like a nun's wimple greeted her enthusiastically. Straight ahead there were signs hanging from the ceiling, in all likelihood indicating the various teas available. An L-shaped counter closed off the space. At the back, a tall vertical sign with calligraphy overlooked the aisles where employees were busy weighing and wrapping. On the right, an illuminated window display exhibited utensils, boxes of tea, and a precious little jar whose price seemed to Rose out of all proportion. She jumped when someone came to speak to her in English. Close up, the young woman's kerchief distracted her, and she didn't understand what she was saying.

"*Okyakusama* needs help?" said the young woman again.

"Oh," said Rose. "The tea room, please?"

The young woman smiled, pointed to the back of the shop, and motioned to her to turn right. Beth Scott was waiting for her, reading, her back against the sand-finished wall. The tables were made of the same old, dark wood that gave its patina to the house. Partitions of a lighter wood, ornamented with an openwork of vertical lines, added a contemporary note. Oddly enough, the conjunction of these more modern elements and the cast iron kettle and bamboo utensils behind the counter made it seem to Rose as if time were being stretched, and fervor lost. On one side the street was visible through a window identical to the ones in her bedroom; on the other side, the glass panes of a picture window opened onto a miniature tableau of plant life, with a maple tree, a fern, and a few azaleas.

Beth Scott looked up at Rose.

"Oh, hello, hello," she said. "I'm so glad to see you again."

And as Rose was taking her seat:

"Are you ready for a mystical experience?"

In the dim light, her face was soft, almost silky.

"Where are we?" Rose asked.

"In the only tea house in town that serves koicha."

They observed each other.

"You've come a long way," said the Englishwoman.

A waitress came over, and Beth ordered, delighting Rose with her way of speaking Japanese. The young woman in her green apron laughed, putting her hand in front of her mouth, then slipped away, shuffling along the floor with the soles of her feet.

"I've just come from Nanzen-ji," Rose said. "My father is having me carted around from one temple to the next; I suppose that counts as coming a long way."

"Nanzen-ji isn't the most beautiful," Beth said, "but it always makes me want to cry."

"I've heard you spend all your time in Zen gardens," Rose said.

"Did Paul say that?" she asked with a laugh.

Rose blushed at hearing Paul's name.

"How did you know my father?"

"I was one of his clients, but we were friends, as well."

"What do you do in life?"

"Various things. I'm a widow, I have money, I love Kyōto, I live here nine months out of the year—what else is there to say?"

There are plenty of other things to say, thought Rose.

"My mother died five years ago," she said. "At the time I thought my father would get in touch with me."

"Five years ago?" Beth repeated. "Haru fell ill five years ago, and after that his illness was long and cruel."

"Everyone here has been ill," said Rose.

"Are you thinking of Clara?" Beth asked.

The waitress set a little oblong green cake down in front of Beth, with a pink and white one for Rose and, in lieu of forks, little bamboo sticks. Rose's plate was streaked with brown and gray lines.

"Eat," said Beth. "It's better to have something in your stomach."

Rose struggled with her little stick, hindered by the soft texture of the confection. Inside was a red paste, sweet on the tongue, exquisitely contrasting with the sugary blandness of the outside.

"What was she like?" Rose asked.

"Clara? Funny, pragmatic, no-nonsense. Paul is secretive, a complex personality. She was his access to life on earth. They laughed a lot together. She loved him very much."

Rose put down her little stick.

"Paul has spent this last decade looking after sick people," said Beth. "He lived exclusively for them, for his daughter, and for his work."

"There haven't been any women in his life since Clara died?"

"There have been women, but I wouldn't go so far as to say they're in his life."

"Women in Tōkyō?" asked Rose, and immediately regretted it.

The tone of Beth Scott's reply was neutral.

"They're not important."

I don't even need anyone's help to make myself look ridiculous, thought Rose, exasperated.

"Clara's funeral was the saddest I've ever been to," Beth continued. "Anna was two years old; Paul could only keep on his feet because she was there. Without her, I think he would have died. He was in hell, and we were at his side, so sorry for him, unable to help."

Rose had a sudden intuition.

"Why does he limp?" she asked.

"That's up to him to tell you," Beth replied.

The waitress brought two bowls on a tray, which she set down on the next table. She turned the first bowl in her palm, placed it in front of Beth, and bowed. It was a lovely pale brown color, decorated with a tastefully executed white rabbit. Rose liked it, but the other bowl enthralled her—its irregularities, gray crackling on a clear glaze, its tortured sobriety, the impertinence of its bold scars.

"This technique of crazed firing comes from the Northern Song Dynasty," Beth said. "Isn't it magnificent? From the utmost simplicity, totally unexpectedly, complexity is born."

Inside each bowl there was a sort of bright green, almost fluorescent paste. Rose tilted her bowl back and forth. The paste hardly moved.

"You drink this?" she asked.

Beth nodded. Rose breathed in the substance, and she recalled the tea at Kōtō-in, the strength that came from nothing, its total power; she drank as if plunging into cold water. The bitterness grabbed her in the stomach and then, immediately afterward, her mouth was filled with a taste of watercress, vegetable, prairie grass—do I like this? she wondered.

Everything became sharper. An awareness of vast green expanses descended into her throat.

"This is the first concentrated matcha of the tea ceremony," Beth said. "Now they will serve you a second, lighter one, adding water to what remains on the side of the bowl."

Rose licked what she could of the residual tea paste. Something drew her back to Nanzen-ji, to the density of time, to a lost sense of the primitive. The waitress came for the bowls. Rose didn't want any more cake, nothing but the bitterness with its blade and its offer of a journey to a forgotten land.

"Last night I dreamed of a large temple with a field of plum trees in front of it," she said.

"That could be Kitano Tenmangū," said Beth, "on Imadegawa, to the west. In February, everyone goes there to admire the flowers."

She pointed to her bowl.

"At the end of the sixteenth century, they had one of the greatest tea ceremonies ever organized for the emperor, with three of the founders of the Way of Tea, including Sen no Rikyū. There were said to be thousands of guests."

All of a sudden, Rose thought of Paul. She shook her head, tried to distract herself.

"Do you have children?" she asked.

Beth ignored her question.

"The revelation of your existence came as a shock," she said. "Just imagine half of Kyōto at the funeral, and Paul reading Haru's letter."

"Letter?" said Rose.

Silence.

"I think the lawyer will pass it on to you," Beth said, finally.

"Everything is being decided without me," Rose murmured.

Beth laughed.

"That's life."

A second tea was brought, with the same taste as the one at Kōtō-in but finer; in it, Rose could make out the scents of the forest on a day of hunting through the undergrowth.

"What did you like about Nanzen-ji?" Beth asked.

Rose took her time to find the right words.

"Something clear, primitive, liquid yet unmoving."

Beth laughed again, appreciatively, but somewhat surprised.

"You two are alike, Paul and you," she said.

"I don't see how," Rose said.

"The sea inside you. That's where you sail."

Beth tilted her head, pensive.

"Haru would have liked it," she added.

She hadn't touched her cake.

"Would you like it?" she asked.

Rose shook her head. Beth smiled.

"I've got to get going now," she said, "but next time I'll take you to another tea house I think you'll like, too."

They parted in the street. Back at Haru's, Rose lay on the futon, overcome by a feeling of unbearable tension—or is this frustration? she wondered. The irises from the day before had been replaced by a pink camellia, and she was struck by its resonance with Nanzen-ji. It's all connected, she thought, but I'm not part of that *all*. Again she saw the still, moving stones, the gray sand, the trees in the moss; every image sent her back to Paul's absence; not knowing why, she could feel great ice floes drifting, liquid shards. After an hour of this shapeless idleness, she stood up, went out into the corridor, stood still, waiting. Finally she turned left, and, level with the dark wooden panels, she slid open a door at random. She entered a cool, bare room. Scattered on the tatami mats were bowls for tea, a few earthenware and lacquer containers, and a little bamboo whisk. On the floor was a brazier topped by a cast iron kettle; in an alcove, a scroll portraying three violets bending toward an icy ground; below it, in a bronze vase, a little branch of bamboo. Through the picture window that opened onto a patio of azaleas, she saw the dying day rime damp leaves with mother-of-pearl. The room was empty, silent—and yet Rose could sense *something living*, an attentive, silent ghost. She went over to a brown bowl with uneven sides, tried to imagine her father in this room, using these utensils, drinking from these superb, humble bowls. Next to the bamboo whisk, a sort of shining handkerchief had been forgotten: a deep, lovely violet, it lay there in languid folds, as if it had just been dropped by an invisible hand, and, for a moment, Rose thought she caught a glimpse of a bending figure, moving slowly, with delicate, fervent gestures. She stood before the scroll in the alcove. Below the flowers, characters had been calligraphed, set out as if for a poem. A few of them, on the upper right-hand side, seemed to morph into birds, released in flight toward the sky; a light mist rose from the frozen ground; the violets *were alive*. A noise outside roused her from her meditation. She went out and closed the door, stirred by a strange reverence.

In the maple room, she found Sayoko sitting at a low table, papers spread out before her, eyeglasses on her nose.

"I'd like to go to Kitsune for dinner," Rose said.

"Now?" asked Sayoko.

She nodded. Sayoko took out her phone, called someone, hung up.

"Kanto-san coming in ten minutes."

"Thank you," said Rose.

And, on impulse:

"I need to write a letter."

Sayoko got to her feet and went to take a sheet of paper and an envelope from a little desk. Rose sat down next to her, took

the pen Sayoko held out to her, and lost herself in discon-
nected thoughts. Then she wrote: *I would like you to tell me
about my father.* Finally, holding her breath: *I miss you.* She
folded the paper, quickly, sealed the envelope, and handed it to
Sayoko, saying, For Paul; then, appalled, she fled into the garden.

8

During the Northern Song Dynasty in China, when poetry, painting, and calligraphy developed in unison, tucked like jewels in the dreams of ancient wise men, there was a particular fondness for representing and versifying flowers and landscapes. One of the greatest landscape artists of that era had a granddaughter who would beg him every day to draw her a camellia. For an entire decade, she pleaded on behalf of her flower. At the age of fifteen, she died one night from a galloping affliction. At dawn, Fan Kuan painted a camellia damp with his tears, and beneath it he inscribed a poem of petals flown away. Finally, gazing at the still-damp scroll, he saw, to his terror, that it was his finest work.

A Camellia Damp with His Tears

As they were pulling up next to Kitsune's red lantern, she no longer knew why she had wanted to come. Kanto sat at the bar; she sat opposite, at a table for six. The yakitori restaurant was deserted. The chef came to see her. Same as last time but beer only, she said. He returned to his stove. He'd shown no emotion. She drank her first beer in one go and looked around her. She saw new details. On the counter, in front of the sake bottles, was an old rotary telephone; enameled advertising plaques were diligently rusting; some of the manga posters were torn. What sort of man had Haru been, to enjoy coming to a place like this? she wondered. On a wave of resentment, she ordered another beer. She felt lonely and blind, faulted herself for a surfeit of sentimentality, and hated herself for having hoped—hoped what? she thought, ordering a third beer. Kanto had his back to her, was placidly talking with the chef; she could sense his respectful vigilance, and it exasperated her. The workings of death, the workings of the liquid stones, the letter she had written to Paul—all seemed ridiculous to her now. She nibbled on her meat skewers with the same resentment. When she asked for a fourth beer, she saw the chef glance at Kanto. The driver made a little gesture that signified, I'll deal with it, and she was mortified. Later, when she wanted to get to her feet, he came to hold her by the shoulders. She did not protest, let herself be led to the car. In the little garden, she motioned to him that she would continue by herself; he didn't insist. She found herself in the darkened maple room; it was gently vibrating, the branches heavy with night; the trees of Nanzen-ji, painful and sharp, abraded her memory. She went to her room, got undressed. Naked, raw, she looked out the window, wiped her hand over her brow, noticed a piece of paper on the futon. She deciphered it in the dark, on her knees. *Paul-san coming tomorrow at 7:30. I wake you at 7:00, Sayoko.*

She fell onto the tatami, her arms flung across her chest. A ladleful of stars shone through the clouds; from the river came a strange monotonous chant; she was awake for a long time, not moving. Somewhat later she awoke, shivering, dragged herself onto her futon, wrapped herself in the light sheet. The night was shining; she felt the presence of secret spirits, of a life of semidarkness heaving with sighs; she recalled her arrival, the magnolia flowers splattered with light, the presence, already then, of spirits. Everything is the same, everything is in mutation, she thought. A corolla was expanding, she felt terrified. She drifted off into a dreamless sleep. Three short knocks on her door startled her awake. She sat up and saw it was light out. Her head was splitting. It's seven o'clock, came Sayoko's voice on the other side of the door. I'm getting ready, mumbled Rose. She mistook the soap for the shampoo, couldn't do her hair, put on a wrinkled dress, swapped it for a skirt and blouse that didn't go together. In the mirror she looked like an unfinished thing. She put on some lipstick, hastily scrubbed it off with a cotton ball, went to the maple room. Paul and Sayoko looked at her and laughed. She stood still, nonplussed.

"What's wrong?" she asked.

Sayoko took three short steps over to her, removed a handkerchief from her sky blue obi, and wiped Rose's cheek. Rose met her gaze, read discreet compassion in her expression. Sayoko took a step back, considered her work, laughed again, and pointed to her blouse.

"You've put it on inside out," said Paul. "Is it a new concept? Is it meant to go with the lipstick on your cheek?"

He was smiling. He looked tired, amused. She told herself that he was tall, with a fair complexion—tall and tired, she thought, I'm wearing him out.

"Do I have time to get changed?" she asked.

"It would be a pity; you've already lit up my dreary day."

"I have a splitting headache," she said.

He said a few words to Sayoko, who motioned to Rose to follow her to the kitchen. There she sat her down like a child, handed her a glass of water and a white tablet, which Rose swallowed obediently. Rose-san eat something? asked Sayoko. She declined, put her blouse on the right way, left the kitchen, and followed Paul to the vestibule. They went through the garden. By the gate, she turned and saw Sayoko bow, then give them a little wave. Rose lowered her head and climbed into the car.

"Forgive me for getting you up so early," said Paul, "but we have to be at the temple when it opens. After that it really will be too busy."

"I thought you were staying in Tōkyō today," she said.

"I got back early this morning. After dinner, I stopped by the apartment, had a shower, and caught the four A.M. Shinkansen."

"You have an apartment in Tōkyō?"

"It's Haru's."

"You didn't get any sleep?"

"No," he said. "I was having dinner with clients. A very long dinner."

He laughed.

"No serious transactions are ever made in Japan without a long dinner and a great deal of sake."

She wondered if he'd received her letter, imagined him on a station platform, lost in his thoughts without a single one for her. His presence next to her was disturbing; she remembered taking his hand, two days ago; now the thought of it horrified her. He didn't say anything, watched the streets fly past. The car stopped in a parking lot already crowded with three bus-loads of visitors. She followed him down a long leafy walkway lined with little shops, waited for him by the ticket office, kept close on his heels along a path next to a large pond with lily pads that seemed unpleasantly picturesque to her—this is a tourist trap, she thought, then: I'm a load of dirty washing being carted around from one laundry to the next. They left the banks of the pond, climbed a few stone steps beneath an archway of indolent maples, came to the entrance of the temple, removed their shoes, took a left behind other visitors, and found themselves before the garden.

"Ryōan-ji," Paul said.

She looked at the large rectangle of stones and sand and felt nothing. And then, as if struck by a sudden backdraft, she let herself slip to the floor of the wooden gallery, crushed by *matter*. Maple and cherry branches cascaded down the walls of the enclosure from outside. Beyond, the foliage formed a bushy, exuberant screen. Inside, there was only sand streaked with parallel lines and seven stones of differing sizes, ellipses raked around them—but Rose was only looking at the walls with their sloping roofs, gray ridge tiles, and bark surface. Ocher and moiré, with the patina of an Italian palazzo, they reflected the gold of the layers of moss surrounding the stones.

"Have the walls always been this color?" she asked.

"No," Paul said. "I think they were white, originally."

"They make the garden," she said.

He seemed surprised.

"The stones have been set out in such a way that you can never see all of them in one gaze," he said.

She tried to concentrate on the rocks and the sand, her spirit strayed, returned to the fresco of the walls.

"There's no end of commentary on Ryōan-ji," he added.

"Have you read it?"

"Some of it, for work."

"And did you learn anything?"

"Did you learn anything from reading your botany books?" he asked.

She didn't like the question.

"I suppose so," she said.

And yet I'm not looking at the flowers, she thought. In search of consolation, she went back to the *matter*.

"Haru was tough when it came to business, and loyal in friendship," Paul said.

He got my note, she thought. Something reeled inside her, the substance of the walls caught her.

"When I met him, he said: I have a great deal of taste but no talent. Over the years I understood that this was his strength: he knew exactly who he was."

She tried to concentrate on the ellipses around the first three stones, could not focus her attention.

"That is what drew so many people to him."

Rose let her gaze return to the golden walls.

"He was Japanese in his habits but atypical in his thoughts. I believe he also liked to have me around because he needed a foreign listener, who would be receptive to unorthodox concepts."

"About what?"

"About women, for example. Japanese women have not had a feminist movement like ours, but Haru was a feminist, in his way. He didn't organize evenings that were for men only. At his place women took part in the discussions."

"Is that why he had kids from casual affairs with foreign women?" she asked, and knowing this was childish of her, she bit her lip.

He did not comment.

"His finest character trait was that he knew how to give. Most people give in order to receive, out of a sense of duty, or because it's the done thing, a sort of automatic reflex. But Haru gave because he understood the significance of giving."

She got a whiff of something like danger; she stared at the wall, and her gaze was suddenly drawn to a stone. Almost level with the sand, smaller than the others, it was sailing across a boundless sea.

"The last months, when Clara was very ill, every evening Haru and I would talk. I went to see him in his study, we drank sake, he listened to me and talked to me. I never got the feeling that it was an effort for him. I don't know if two men have ever known greater complicity."

He fell silent, and she understood that he didn't want to go on. Behind them, a troop of noisy Chinese visitors caused the floor of the gallery to tremble.

"Ryōan-ji doesn't inspire you?" he asked.

"It looks like a giant kitty litter box."

He burst out laughing and, for a split second, was transformed. That's who Paul used to be, before, she thought, the man killed by his wife's death. They stayed there for a moment in silence. Reading a text of rock and sand, Rose let her gaze wander from the stone that had first caught her eye to the others; the scene, too, was transformed; she studied the walls, no longer saw there what she thought she had seen. She went back to the dryness of the rectangle of sand, detected a vibration in *time*—time of birth, time of suffering, time of death, she thought. She looked at Paul. He had closed his eyes, and she recalled his tears at the cemetery. The sense of danger grew, at the same time as a friendly presence, a quiver of hope. And so, looking at the walls made ocher through the grace of years, she knew they only remained standing thanks to the strength of the garden, that its flowerless mineral nature transmuted time into eternity, and that, through this metamorphosis of the hours, no act could ever have the same significance; finally, for some unknown reason, the way Sayoko had waved earlier came back to her—in the solitude of the stones lost in sand, there was a gift. What gift? she wondered, examining the scene. What can such dry, bare space give? She let her spirit wander to the whim of the notes the seven stones played on their score, again felt they were drowning her in a timeless ocean, and that the garden, by itself, *was giving*.

Paul got up, and she followed, focusing on his uneven, flowing gait. In the car, she could see that he was tired.

"And now?" she asked.

"I'm taking you back to Haru's."

"We're not having lunch together?"

"I have to go and get Anna; she came back last night," he said.

"You came back for Anna?" she asked.

He didn't seem to have heard.

"And for the last temple visits before the lawyer visit, of course," she added.

"I came back for you," he said. "I was missing my professional pain in the ass."

He leaned toward Kanto, said something that caused the driver to nod, then made a short phone call in Japanese. The drive took a long time, in a silence that made her feel fragile. In the center of town, in a wide street with arcades, they got out of the car. Paul slipped into an entrance, climbed a flight of stairs. She could sense his fatigue, the pain in his hip. He opened a door, and they were in an ultra-modern room with white tables and apple-green chairs. Behind the counter, large posters depicted waffles with an extravagant variety of toppings. He sat down with relief, and she took the chair opposite him.

"Waffles?" she asked.

"Don't forget I *am* Belgian."

The door opened behind her. He smiled and stood up, his energy regained. Rose turned around and saw a suntanned little girl hurrying toward them. She paused briefly on seeing Rose, then threw herself into her father's arms. She was accompanied by a Japanese woman who must have been in her forties and who came forward shyly. With his arm around his daughter's shoulders, Paul greeted her, and they exchanged a few words with a laugh. Rose had stood up. Anna's face fascinated her.

"Anna, this is Rose," Paul said.

The girl looked at her gravely, went closer, stood on tiptoes, and kissed her on the cheek.

"Are you Haru's daughter?" she asked.

"So it seems," replied Rose.

Anna studied her intensely, her mouth closed, her brow creased.

"Rose, I'd like to introduce Megumi," said Paul, "the mother of Anna's friend Yōko."

The Japanese woman bowed, gave a smile, and said a few hesitant words.

"She welcomes you to Kyōto. She asks how long you are planning to stay."

"I don't know," said Rose. "I'm doing as I'm told."

Again, Anna's sharp gaze. Paul translated something that seemed to satisfy Megumi; she took her leave of them with a bow; at the door, she turned around and made the same gesture as Sayoko. The waitress came to take their order, Anna began chattering, and Paul listened, smiling. The waffles arrived, the little girl pounced on hers, while Rose gazed warily at her own construction of pastry, green coulis, and red grains.

"Don't you like waffles?" Anna asked, her mouth full.

"I'm not sure I like the looks of this weird green concoction from Mars," she answered.

The little girl burst out laughing and looked at her father.

Rose was surprised to see that she was so dark and olive-skinned where he was blond and pale; in addition, she was small and delicate, fine of feature, her nose slightly upturned, her irises dark and shining. She must be the spitting image of her mother, thought Rose. Between voracious mouthfuls, Anna told them about her holidays, laughed, intermittently stared at Rose; and Rose sensed her vigilance, her patient, meticulous watchfulness; I used to be like that, she recalled. Anna begged Paul to order another waffle, looked to Rose for support, radiated with triumph when he yielded. Then suddenly she turned serious.

"Where do you live?" she asked.

"In Paris," answered Rose, "but I also have a house in Touraine."

"Where's that?"

"A little bit farther south."

"Do they have stories there?"

"Stories?"

"Stories about the fairies and sprites that live there?"

The little girl was looking her in the eye. Do I want to be any part of this? wondered Rose. She looked at Paul. The crease in his brow had deepened; she saw that he was concerned. Anna was waiting.

"Yes," she said finally. "My grandmother knew all of them, particularly the ones about merry devils."

"Will you tell them to me?" asked Anna.

Rose's heart, tugged like a weed, was for a split second between two worlds; then the stones of Ryōan-ji entered the circle dance—their starkness, their stony solitude, the certainty of their unspeaking text: the proof offered by deprivation. Something shifted, on the back of a sharp pain.

"I'll tell you all of them," she said.

Anna smiled at her. I'm a butterfly being pinned alive, thought Rose. Paul stood up and went to pay. She could tell he was relieved. Kanto was waiting for them at the foot of the stairs.

"You're off duty now," Paul said to her. "I have to go with Anna to the dentist's, and then I've got to take some clients out to dinner. I'll come for you tomorrow morning; Kanto is at your disposal today."

"And you?" she asked.

"I live just nearby," he said, pointing to the buildings in the city center. "Where do you want to go?"

"I have to go back and get changed first."

He said a few words to Kanto, she got in the car, Anna leaned over and kissed her on the cheek again. Rose met Paul's gaze and saw a shadow of sadness. She would have liked to take his arm, keep him there, pull him toward her. He closed the door. As the car was pulling away, Anna waved her hand energetically, and Rose answered with the same gesture Sayoko had made. When they got to Haru's, she went up to her room, dropped to the floor, and spent the rest of the morning there. The pink camellia was resplendent with jaunty and melancholy flames, and she was drawn into a contemplative mood, something inside her stirring relentlessly.

Later, she got changed, went to the deserted maple room, knocked on the door to the kitchen, and went in. Sayoko and a young woman in a housedress were drinking tea. They brought her coffee and a bowl of rice, and she waited, sitting on the tatami. The two women were having an animated conversation, and Rose listened, relieved not to have to speak, glad she didn't understand. She drank her coffee, ate the rice, wanted to leave. Sayoko motioned to her to wait, rummaged in her handbag, which was on a shelf, took out a telephone, and handed it to her. Code zero zero zero zero, she said. Number one is Paul-san, number two is Sayoko, number three is Kanto-san. Rose took the telephone, went back up to her room, and lay down again. A mighty downpour was darkening the world, the camellia shone in flashes with the shimmering of the rain. After a while, Rose went out, and, in the corridor, on impulse, she opened the sliding door that was opposite the tea room. She went into a tatami room that looked out on the river. The only furnishing was a hospital bed, poised in the space like a spider; a large abstract painting hung opposite; a black vase stood on a lacquered night table. In the rain-light, the scene seemed to be in motion, uncertain. In response to the bleary stain of the mattress, the painting emanated a vibrant power, an immense carmine stain drowning in a flat tint of deep ink. But although it had neither lines nor contours, Rose was convinced it represented a flower: a camellia, a lotus, perhaps a rose. Did he die here? she wondered and, going closer, she reached out to touch the bare mattress. She held her breath, hesitated, stepped back. An indefinable scent mingling cedar, aniseed, and violet drifted through the room. Shadows seemed to linger there, and for a moment she thought she could feel a breath on the back of her neck. The harshness of the metal bed unsettled her, just as another sensation was working its way through her. Suddenly, she was seized by the absolute certainty that the corolla *was alive*, despite the power of death. She thought of Anna, her shining eyes, the merry devils, the wave she'd given her as the car was pulling away. And then again she saw the garden of sand and stone, surrounded by walls of gold, and thought: The walls are nothing without the garden; our time on earth is nothing without the eternity of giving.

9

We are told that one morning, Sen no Rikyū was washing the stones on the path to his tea house with clear water when a young fox emerged from the nearby trees and stopped to wait under the foliage of a tall heavenly bamboo. After a moment where they observed each other in silence, the little fox carefully tore off a branch of bamboo and went to leave it on a flat stone where the guests for that evening's ceremony would be sure to step. When his young disciple expressed his surprise that his master let it stay there, in the way of the guests, Sen no Rikyū said to him: The fox and the bamboo teach us how to make detours.

The Bamboo Teaches Us How to Make Detours

At three o'clock, Rose decided to go out. In the maple room, she found Sayoko busy arranging a bouquet of magnolia branches. She explained that she was going out, but Sayoko left her flowers, went to fetch a little purse with a pattern of pink clouds from a low table, and handed it to her, saying, Money for stroll. Rose thanked her with a wave of her hand, Sayoko smiled, and she smiled back, undecided. As she was about to turn and go out, Sayoko took a photograph from her belt and held it out to her. Surprised, Rose took it. It pictured Sayoko and three other women with the same gentle face; the only difference was the color and cut of their gray or black hair; each one had pearly skin, a pure oval face; they were laughing, sitting on tatami mats in front of a mountain setting.

"My sisters," Sayoko said.

Rose was speechless. The print was creased, she imagined Sayoko must look at it often. Curious, she studied the sisters' features. Dutiful women, she thought, but their laughter is lively.

"You need one," Sayoko added.

Rose nodded, handed back the photograph. In the vestibule, she reached for an umbrella. It was raining, steady showers, but the sky had lightened and the sun was visible through the cutout of clouds. She went to the river; motionless herons stood guard, scattered along the banks. She walked as far as the bridge from the second day, turned left in front of the entrance to the covered gallery, walked for a while under the arcades on the street where the waffle restaurant was. An automatic door opened on her right and let out an insane burst of noise. She went into a vast room with harsh neon lights, did not understand what she was looking at. Men and women sat staring vacantly at multicolored slot machines. The noise was unbelievable, the ugliness indescribable; this, she thought, is hell, the real hell, Haru's antiworld. She fled from the absurdity of this crazy, sick Japan, and made her way back to the covered gallery, turned right toward the main road, crossed it, and continued north. After a few yards, the street regained some charm, lined with refined boutiques. She went into one, admired the ceramics displayed on wooden shelves, bowls like her father's; everything was magnificent. She went closer to a shallow bowl that had the texture of rice, white with irregular patches that intermittently caught the light; next to it she saw a photograph of a man in front of a potter's wheel. She wondered if he was one of Haru's artists, worked out the price of the piece, figured that it wasn't expensive enough. She went back out, walked up the street, looked in the windows at brushes, paper, lacquer. She felt incongruous, at a loose end; Kyōto wasn't expecting her, didn't know her, she was wandering aimlessly, feeling useless and futile. She thought of Sayoko, of the four sisters, their smiling faces—prisoners, but luminous, she mused, and she felt more out of touch than ever. Before long, on the right, she recognized the tea house from the fluttering banners with their ideograms. Everything that had previously seemed graceless here in the town center touched her now—the little buildings, the peaceful streets, the elegant boutiques—she understood at last how they were a continuation of those admirable gardens. Beth Scott's words came back to her: gardens where gods come to take tea. A country for merry devils, more like, she thought; even at the heart of the sublime, you're in the company of the child you used to be.

She went into the tea house, let herself be led to a table on the other side of the room. She ordered in English, and the waitress in the green apron gave a smile. Which koicha? asked the young woman. Rose was flustered. They showed her the menu, there were two sorts, she chose the least expensive. With the first pulpy swallow, she thought of Paul, his absence, his unfathomable sadness. She couldn't stand the thought that she would have to wait until tomorrow to see him again. I'm a pile of dirty laundry abandoned on the empty counter, she thought again. She took another swallow of koicha, and suddenly Anna's face was everywhere—her attentive eyes, eager for stories of sprites, the thought that she didn't have her father's features, that she looked like her mother. Rose finished her bowl, waited for the next one, drank quickly, comforted by the affability of the lighter tea. She took out the telephone Sayoko had given her, struggled for a moment with the keys, found the contacts, pressed the third one, and waited. When she heard Kanto's voice, she said, I am at the tea house, can you come? Ten minutes, he replied. She paid and went out to wait on the sidewalk. It had stopped raining, the air smelled of tar.

Kanto arrived and turned to her once she was in the car. Can we go to Nanzen-ji? she asked. Closed now, he replied. She looked at her phone. It was six o'clock. Home then, she said. In the deserted maple room, an urge came over her to lie down and sleep beneath the foliage. She gave a start when her phone rang. She opened it, saw *Paul* on the screen. She answered, her heart pounding.

"Are you too tired for a drink after dinner?" she heard him ask.

"No," she replied.

"Will you be in town?"

"I'll be at Haru's."

"I'll come by for you as soon as I've finished with my clients."

She went to her room, took a bath, put on a flowered dress, lipstick, pinned up her hair, resisted the impulse to remove her makeup, went back to the big room. The maple was swaying slightly. She lay down on a low sofa and enjoyed the sensation of capsizing. Before long, she fell asleep. In the depths of her hazy dreams, a fairy was flying, a fairy with Anna's face; she glided across the sky, then landed on Rose's shoulder and said her name. Rose awoke and, opening her eyes, saw Paul leaning over her. She sat up, disoriented. His gaze was kind, but then all of a sudden he laughed.

"You clearly have a problem with lipstick," he said.

She ran her hand over her cheek, and he laughed again.

"Maybe you should use a mirror," he suggested.

She went into the bathroom and saw that lipstick had run down from the right corner of her lips. I was drooling, she thought, aghast. She removed her makeup, took a step toward the door, changed her mind, applied the lipstick again, and adjusted her hair. Back in his presence, she could tell from the way he looked at her that he thought she was beautiful. She followed him out to the car through the moist air, under a moon draped with mist. Someone called him on the phone, the conversation in Japanese lasted a long time; she could hear the fatigue in his voice, could sense his reserve, the restraint in his body. He hung up; she couldn't stand the silence and stirred in her seat.

"Have you ever thought of moving back to Belgium?" she asked.

He turned to her. In the gloom of the car, his expression was grave, the wrinkle on his brow accentuated. His pale skin was like a mask.

"Belgium?"

His phone rang again. He ignored it.

"All I wanted when I came to Japan was to live in Kyōto and be surrounded by a certain type of art and culture. Haru gave me that possibility. Death finished rooting me here."

She wanted to change the subject, to say, You haven't slept in two days, you must be exhausted, but the car was already pulling over on a street in the center of town. They got out, went up a short flight of steps to an anonymous door, and entered a large, dark room lit in places by sparkling cones. Along the wall on the left, a line of heavenly bamboo burst from a bed of gray pebbles. On the right, customers were drinking at a counter in front of sake cellars illuminated like chapels. Joyful cries greeted their entrance; from a table at the far end of the room, five men waved their arms at Rose and Paul, and Rose recognized one of them.

"The drunken potter," she murmured.

"But with his gang, which is even more formidable," said Paul. "Alas, there's no going back now."

"Who are the others?"

"A photographer, a producer for the national television, a musician, and a French colleague of mine, all of them three sheets to the wind at this point."

"One of your colleagues?"

"A Parisian antique dealer, to be more precise."

They went closer, and Rose suddenly felt lighter. I'll drink, she thought—after all, why shouldn't I? The Japanese men's gaze on her was kindly, Keisuke Shibata had a mocking smile on his lips. She met his eyes. This is the night for a showdown, she thought, astonished by the unusual thought. The Frenchman, a hairy man in his fifties wearing a cashmere sweater and a polka dot *lavallière*, doffed an invisible hat.

"Are you French, Mademoiselle?" he asked.

She nodded. He let out a quiet whistle.

"Forgive me for not standing," he said, "but I'm not really up to it just now. As for my Japanese friends, they're all barbarians, they don't stand in the presence of women."

He seemed to reflect for a moment.

"Although I am the only gay one here."

Then, pouring himself another drink:

"Which has nothing to do with it."

Rose and Paul sat down, the Japanese noisily called for more sake, Rose downed her first cup in one go.

"My name is Édouard," said the antique dealer, whom she was sitting next to. "And you are—"

"Rose."

Keisuke said her father's name with a chuckle.

"Oh, so you're Haru's daughter?"

"Among other things," she replied.

"And otherwise?" he asked.

"I'm a botanist."

"And apart from that?"

Apart from that? she wondered.

"I'm a pain in the ass."

He laughed and embarked on a conversation about everything and nothing, and, with the help of the sake, she graciously joined in. The evening continued in this vein: she drank, she chatted with Édouard, she laughed, and, after an hour, she knew she was dead drunk. It seemed to her they'd been talking about flowers, and restaurants, and love, and betrayal—but her gaze, for a while now, had been returning to the heavenly bamboo, one branch of which, lower than the others, was caressing the wooden floor; it looked like a rebellious feather on the smooth plumage of a pale green bird; having slipped from the ranks, now blocking the way, it was shouting something at the top of its chlorophyll lungs. Across from her, Paul was conversing with his neighbors; Keisuke, at regular intervals, cried out for more sake.

"What are they talking about?" she asked Édouard.

"Politics."

The conversations gradually slackened off. During a lull, Keisuke jerked his chin in her direction.

"He says you seem to have defrosted a little," said Paul.

The poet was looking at her, she could read the irony in his eyes and, to her astonishment, immense kindness.

"He says you're pretty but you don't smile, in addition to being too thin."

The drunkard added a few words that made the others laugh.

"And now?" asked Rose.

"Something intended for me, which I won't translate," he replied.

In Japanese this time, Paul told a story where she could clearly make out the name *Ryōan-ji*, and they all burst out laughing. Édouard patted her on the back.

"I shared the fact that you compared Ryōan-ji to a giant litter box," said Paul.

Keisuke shouted something, slapping the table, and the guests agreed, nodding their heads in unison.

"Fucking Zen priests," Paul translated.

The potter turned morose again.

"Ryōan-ji, the end of the world," Paul translated.

Then, as no explanation followed, they all resumed their conversations, and Rose went back to chatting with Édouard. At one point, when Paul went over to say hello to some acquaintances at the entrance to the room, she asked her new friend what it was Paul hadn't wanted to translate earlier on.

"Oh, with pleasure," he laughed. "Keisuke said to him: You should give her a nice fuck, that would finish defrosting her."

He looked at Paul.

"Personally, I wouldn't say no," he added.

And, as Paul was heading back toward their table:

"I didn't tell you anything."

Silence fell again, and Keisuke pointed a finger at Rose. Ah, she thought, the showdown. He began speaking, and Paul got up and took a chair from the next table and sat behind Rose. He translated simultaneously; she could feel his breath on her neck.

"Your father was the spirit of a samurai in the body of a merchant, a bastard of an exploiter, but he paid well, and, above all, he was a loyal friend. Paul belongs to the same race, less brutal, but cleverer. And as he's Belgian, the Japanese don't see him coming. He learned from his master, he was his disciple, his confidant, his doctor, his friend."

He paused. From time to time, Rose looked at the branch of bamboo, behind the potter. She was struck by its lack of symmetry, its rebellious languor.

"Do you know what a friend is?" continued Keisuke.

"A dead man?" she suggested.

He guffawed, once Paul had translated.

"Your father said: A friend is a person you would be glad to find yourself shipwrecked with. Mountain folk are dead stupid, but when everything's collapsing around you, the only person you want by your side is an imbecile like that. And you? Are you both admirable and stupid to that degree, as well?"

"No," she said, "I'm French."

He exploded with laughter.

"You really are your father's daughter," he croaked.

Someone walked past the bamboo branch, making a detour around it, and Rose was enthralled. Keisuke asked Paul a question, and he answered with one word.

"Did you know your father liked flowers?" asked the drunkard. "But you're an idiot botanist, you stick labels on them, so basically you don't give a damn."

She looked him in the eyes and saw only tenderness. For whom? she wondered. For him? For me?

"Your father, at least, knew how to look at them," continued Keisuke.

"All the flowers except Rose," she said.

He was following a train of thought and ignored her remark.

"Are you specialized in anything?"

"Geographical botany."

"You follow the trail of flowers?" he asked.

"In a way."

He giggled.

"It's high time to find them."

He poured some more sake.

"*A single rose is every rose*," he said. "That's Rilke, nothing to do with your useless science. Do you think your father didn't look at roses? He lived his life as a merchant and never understood women at all, but he was a samurai, he knew that straight lines are fatal."

Rose went back to the bamboo branch. Something was tickling her intuition, slipping away, then knocking again at the door of her consciousness.

"If straight lines are fatal to men, then why not to women?" Paul translated. "If you don't understand that, you might as well go straight to hell."

The potter snorted noisily, wiped his nose on the sleeve of his jacket.

"You're young, you can afford to take a different path. Afterward, it will be too late."

He seemed on the point of adding something, then gave up. He looked at Paul.

"You yourself know it very well, ashes, ashes . . . "

He made a gesture of weariness, put his head between his hands, murmured a few words.

"What did he say?" Rose asked.

"After ashes, roses," said Paul.

His voice was husky. I arrived after the battle was over, she thought, they went through the end of the world together, I will never be part of that bond. Paul sat back down on the other side of the table; she felt abandoned.

"Does Keisuke say *tu* to me?" she asked Édouard.

"They don't really have *tu* and *vous* in Japanese the way we do in French, but he speaks to you the way he would if you were his daughter, with the informal pronouns that are the equivalent of saying *tu* in French."

"As if I were his daughter?" she echoed. "Now I've got one dead man and one drunkard for putative fathers."

"He lost his three children," Édouard pointed out, obligingly. "You can't hold it against him for being daft enough to want to adopt a French pain in the ass."

After a while, Paul stood up and took his leave of the gathering. He seemed exhausted, and she followed obediently. By the entrance, she sidestepped around the rebellious bamboo branch, and she got the distinct impression that she was taking a path less travelled she'd long known and long forgotten; she paused for a moment, struck by this detour in a place without matter or substance. Outside, she breathed deeply. The air smelled of summer, Kanto was waiting for them, standing in the dark, silent, unreal. As she was climbing in the car, she suddenly turned back and found herself just inches from Paul. He moved in surprise, stepping back slightly. She felt drunk but strangely vigilant.

"Don't you want to . . . " she murmured.

She put her hand on his forearm. He took her by the shoulders and propelled her gently into the car, like a child. She wanted so badly for him to want—for him to want what? She was lost in thought.

"You've drunk enough for a regiment," he said, "and I'm not very sober myself."

He leaned toward her.

"I'll pick you up tomorrow morning; we'll be going to another part of town. And after that to the lawyer's."

"What will happen there?" she asked.

"He'll tell you what Haru has left to you."

She wanted to reply: What does it matter, what he's left to me? But behind Paul, in the narrow view from the street to the river, she saw that beneath the moon great bands of mist were rising. She thought about her renegade bamboo, its vitality as a fugitive, how it insisted on breaking away—somewhere in her skull, Keisuke's voice was murmuring *different path*, and she heard herself say:

"I'll accept it."

Before he closed the door, she saw the flare of emotion on his face—the real Paul, she thought—then the car slid away in the night. Going into Haru's house now felt like a homecoming. From her room, she swore allegiance to the mists rising toward the mountains and the monsoon sky, toward the red moon. She fell asleep, a deep sleep, woke briefly, looked through the window for the moon and found it, huge and tawny, veined with dark branches.

10

At the very end of the Ming Dynasty, the future painter Shitao, then only three years old, lost his entire family, murdered by a rival faction in the court of the Chongzhen Emperor. A servant saved him from the massacre and led him to the Buddhist monks of Mount Xiang. There, he learned calligraphy. Later, he set out into the world to fulfill his destiny as an artist.

Shitao, a name that means *stone wave*, was so good at representing rocks that you would have sworn they were alive, but his true passion was moss. However, he never depicted it on his scrolls. One day, when his friend the painter Zhū Dā asked him why this was so, he replied: Moss caresses stone like a loving woman, and soon, perhaps, I will manage to paint it—and then, far from battle, I will make my art into a story about love.

In the early morning, it was pouring. The world was fading away, the river was vibrating. Rose knelt on the tatami and saw that a tray had been left there with a glass of water and a white pill. She figured that Paul had called Sayoko, that they had talked about her and he had left instructions. A wave of shapeless desire ran through her. She took the pill, lay down. *He knew exactly who he was.* She tried to recall the conversation, its setting, its texture. How does one know who one is? she wondered. The walls of gold came back to her—the stones, their sudden presence, their silent offering. What was the name of that garden? Ryōan-ji, she thought, with a sense of triumph. Then, with a sentiment of bitterness: I don't exist, I cannot know who I am.

She took a shower and got dressed; every movement was painful; she lay down again, waited for the migraine to dissipate, and saw that the camellia was gone. After a moment, she went into the main room and found Sayoko, wearing the brown kimono from the first day with her peony obi. Sitting at a low table, she was writing in an accounts book. She got up, went into the kitchen, and reappeared with the morning tray. While Rose was struggling with an entire fish, Sayoko went on with her bookkeeping. The sound of rain on the moss of the maple was duller than usual. Rose finished her breakfast, thought of going out, changed her mind.

"No flowers in my room today?" she asked.

Sayoko smiled.

"Paul-san want you choose."

Surprised, Rose remained silent. Sayoko studied her for a moment, serious and concentrated.

"Paul-san secret man," she said finally.

And as Rose was looking at her, even more surprised:

"Very brave. He know flowers."

What does that have to do with it? thought Rose. And me? Am I brave?

"Rose-san want which flower?" asked Sayoko.

She felt a bit lost.

"In France, I like lilac," she said.

"We have lilac in Japan," said Sayoko. "*Rairakku*. Good season now."

They heard the front door slide open, and Paul came into the room; Rose took his smiling face and pensive gaze straight to her heart; he is handsome, she thought. He said a few words to Sayoko, who left the room with hurried little steps.

"Were you able to get some rest?" he asked.

"Yes, but I have a headache," she replied. "And you?"

"I slept like a log; I'm a new man."

Sayoko came back with coffee. Paul drank his slowly, while Sayoko spoke volubly to him and Rose waited, watching them, sensing a furtive life unfolding inside her then vanishing. Finally they looked at her, and Sayoko gave a little nod.

"Are you ready?" asked Paul. "Today we have to keep to the schedule."

In the car, his nearness unsettled her. He still seemed tired, a bit absent.

"Where are we going?" she asked.

"The other side of town, Arashiyama."

"Does that mean something?"

"Storm mountain."

"Which temple?"
"Saihō-ji."

They drove a long way west, in silence, not looking at each other. The city changed, became dreary, impersonal, devoid of the charm of the center; they went down streets crowded with anonymous buildings and ugly neon; the thought that all she'd seen of Japan was six temples and a cemetery was upsetting. Finally, they went down a narrow street, past tall bamboo plants, through a zone that felt almost like countryside. Other visitors were already waiting by the entrance. It was raining. After a few minutes, a monk in a black robe with a collar lined in white came to open the gate. Paul and the others handed him a paper, and everyone followed him to the usual wooden buildings. They were led into a large hall with squat little lecterns where sheets of paper, ink, and brushes were laid out. Paul motioned to Rose to stay at the back and take her place at one of the lecterns. She imitated her Japanese neighbor and sat on her heels, her toes turned slightly inward. Paul folded his legs to one side, trying to hide a grimace. She studied the sheet in front of her, saw ideograms on it, and wanted to ask for an explanation, but just then a procession of monks came in and headed to the center of the hall. Speaking in labored English, a surly-looking superior ordered the assembly to retrace, in ink, the characters of the sūtra there before them. A young monk sat cross-legged in front of a little bench where a shining black bowl stood; another sat by a sculpted wooden fish that rested on a large embroidered cushion. Both of them were holding a slim baton in their hand. Rose yawned.

The three crystal-clear chimes, the dull *pock*, grabbed her in the guts. Sitting up straight, she saw that the first monk was holding his baton away from the shining bowl while the other monk was now tapping the wooden fish, keeping a rapid and regular rhythm. The chant began, a smell of incense rose, the voices were monotonous and fitful. Intermittently, the crystal bowl scanned the recitation. The Japanese woman next to Rose was copying her sūtra, but Rose was caught in a deep flow, intoxicated by a smell of damp earth mingled with dust and blossoms. At last, the monks fell silent. After a moment, during which the tall surly monk said something she did not understand, they were each given a little wooden plaque. The Japanese woman pointed to her brush and said to Rose, Write wish.

"What was that all about?" Rose asked Paul.

"*Hannya shingyō*, the sūtra of the heart," he replied.

"It's about love?"

"It's about emptiness."

"The sūtra of the heart is about emptiness?"

"The sūtra of the heart of wisdom, yes."

She laughed.

"For once I feel I'm where I belong," she said.

He smiled and got to his feet, repressing a grimace. They followed the stream of visitors outside to a gate in a wall and were told something else that Rose did not listen to. At last, they were free. A light drizzle was falling. The chant was still echoing inside her—the crystal-clear scansion, the muffled dullness. They took a paved walkway that wound beneath a cloud of maple trees. It's the undergrowth of a forest, she thought, astonished. Rain filtered in scattered drops from the leaves; everywhere, an extraordinary moss ruled supreme over its private kingdom; thick and moving, poised on root and stone, it seemed to glitter.

"The other name for Saihō-ji is Kokedera, the temple of moss," said Paul.

The moss is enchanted, she thought—rather, the earth is, the earth beneath the moss.

"Haru believed that the earth of Kokedera was magical."

"And you?" she asked, wishing she could say *tu* to him instead of *vous*.

He didn't answer. Then, as they came to a pond lost beneath the foliage:

"For me, this place is full of memories."

Rose looked at the pond. A moss-covered bridge spanned a narrow arm of the pond; a faint vapor skimmed the surface of the water; the shape of the banks spoke to her like writing.

"The humidity from the pond keeps the moss alive," said Paul.

"It has an odd shape," said Rose.

"People say it represents the ideogram for the heart."

He raised his head, looked at the trees.

"That was our last carefree outing."

A wave of sadness swept over Rose. I'm not mourning any-one, she thought. The dull crystal of the sūtra continued to lull her like a heard melody, hummed far away. The moss shone with pearls of rain—monsoon dew, she thought. They contin-ued on their way. Something was rising from the earth, she felt it brushing against her, its secret magic.

"Anna was a year old; I was carrying her on my back," said Paul. "She says she remembers, but I don't see how she could."

The merry devils, thought Rose. They went ahead in silence. When they reached the end of the garden, she looked at the trees rooted in the sweep of velvet; looked at the rain-drops, the kindness of water on plants and of plants on the earth; it's a caress, she thought. The kinship of dew and moss, the fusion of crystal, earth, and wood suddenly made it absolutely clear to her that she had never stopped mourning Paule, that she had been mourning her for years, for centuries of silence. She placed her hand on her heart, and then it all passed, in a fragrance of cemetery, a psalm of black rain.

They left the temple and, after a few miles in the countryside, drove northward along a river until they reached a major bridge of iron and wood in a busy neighborhood with restaurants and colorful shops along the riverbanks. A little farther along, they got out of the car, dipped under a short gray curtain, and found themselves in a tatami room that opened onto a garden of azaleas. Paul ordered, tea and ice cold beer were brought, as well as a lacquered box for each of them and a little wooden container with a curved stick. Rose opened the box and, on a bed of rice, found slices of fish coated with a pale brown sauce.

"Eel," said Paul.

He picked up the little wooden container, scooped out some green powder and sprinkled it on his fish.

"Sanshō."

She tasted the eel. The flesh fell in strips from a gray, oily skin. She was surprised at how sweet the sauce was, how tender the fish, its silky texture, nothing tough or viscous about it, and how well it harmonized with the vinegary rice; she drank her beer, looking at Paul; she was glad of his silence. He finished his lunch, leaned back against the partition, stretched out his legs. With painful intensity, she wanted him to desire her, wanted him to willingly share with her who he was. *Paul is a secretive, a complex personality.* Who said that? she wondered, then, Beth Scott.

"Sayoko doesn't like Beth Scott," she said.

He raised an eyebrow in amusement.

"Beth isn't much liked in Kyōto; she has a reputation for being ruthless in business and not playing by the rules. She doesn't pay much attention to others when her own interests are at stake."

"What sort of business?"

"She inherited her husband's property in real estate and turned it into an empire."

"Her husband was Japanese?"

He nodded.

"She's very clever," he said. "Despite what people think of her, and the fact that she's a foreign woman, she's managed to make a name for herself here. That's quite a feat."

"Do you get along well with her?"

"Very well."

"And did my father?"

She saw him give a faint twitch because she had said *my father*.

"Haru liked her a great deal."

"Why?"

"He liked wounded people."

"She lost a child, didn't she?"

"You're drawing conclusions without many clues to go on," he said.

Puzzled, she shook her head.

"It's not the first time I've noticed that," he added.

There was something strangely gentle in his eyes, she imagined he was thinking of someone else, that he had recently fallen in love with some unknown woman; she panicked at the thought that he was about to disappear from her days, her sight, her life.

"It's time to go to the lawyer's," he said, getting to his feet.

While he was paying at the counter by the door, she noticed that his hip was hurting him. He took a step toward the door, looked over his shoulder while she was still behind him.

"That wasn't a climbing accident," she said.

A shadow of weariness passed over his face.

"No," he said.

She followed him outside. It had started raining again. Kanto said something to Paul that made him take out his phone and make a call in Japanese. She looked around her at the passersby, the transparent umbrellas, the streets running with rainwater. The tenderness of the moss was with her, conflicting with the depths of her sadness. I'm Haru's daughter, she thought, no more than this daughter that Haru told Paul to show around Kyōto. He's known about me for twenty years, he knows who I am, my emptiness, my anger. The sudden knowledge that he had seen her in photographs with her lovers was torture to her. *And all that time, he loved someone, he was suffering because he loved someone.* The car stopped in a street in the center, under a torrential downpour. Kanto came around to open her door and shielded her with an umbrella up to the entrance of a sinister gray building. Paul joined her, held the door open, went ahead of her down a labyrinth of corridors, then through another door. An employee at a reception desk stood up, bowed to them, and led them into an office where an elderly man was waiting for them, along with a young woman who bowed in turn.

"I am your interpreter," she said.

"Can't Paul translate?" asked Rose.

"It's the law," said the young woman. "I'm sorry."

She was very pretty, with clear gray eyes and a profile worthy of a cameo.

"That's fine," said Rose, sorry she had been so abrupt.

Paul exchanged a few friendly words with the lawyer. The man looked like an old frog, with a wide mouth, narrow brow, and a lively, inquisitive gaze; on his lips was a good-natured smile; a peculiar office batrachian, she thought. Everything seemed unreal. I have been appointed to apprise you of your father's last wishes, translated the young woman, and Rose drifted off. She couldn't concentrate anymore, caught snatches of random words and phrases that she didn't grasp, struggled breathlessly in dark, icy waters. At one point, she met Paul's worried gaze. He stood up and came to place his hand on her shoulder; the gentle pressure brought her back to the surface. The lawyer handed her a file; she didn't know what to do with it. Paul took it for her and went on standing next to her. After a moment, the interpreter asked: Did you understand every-thing, do you have any questions? Rose shook her head. The young woman continued: Now there are documents to sign. Rose looked at Paul and murmured: I want to leave. He said a few words to the lawyer, took her by the arm, and led her through the corridors. Under the awning, at the entrance, to the deafening sound of the downpour, she gasped for breath. We're going home, said Paul. In the car, she began to sob uncontrollably. He put his arm around her shoulders, said something to Kanto, who made a quick telephone call, put his lips to her temple, caressed her hair. Everything came apart, she sobbed even harder, like a child. Outside the house, the pain of feeling Paul move away from her was unbearable. Sayoko was waiting for them on the raised floor with a length of fabric in her hands. She wrapped it around Rose and, hold-ing her close, led her into the maple room. On a low table, bowls of tea were steaming; faint incense was burning; Rose collapsed on the floor. Paul spoke in hushed tones, Sayoko nodded her head. He sat down next to her.

"Get some rest; I'll come back later," he said.

Through her tears, she shook her head, but he walked away and, after a final exchange with Sayoko, left the house. Sayoko knelt down, wiped Rose's cheeks with a handkerchief. Abruptly, Rose got up, ran to the hall and out into the garden, barefoot. On the other side of the gate, by the car, Paul was closing his umbrella.

"Don't go," she cried.

He let go of his umbrella, walked back toward her, and while she stood motionless in the cloudburst, he held her close. Sayoko came out, and they led her back inside. Paul bent over her and gently smoothed her hair away from her face.

"I'll be back soon," he said.

"Please," she begged, and took his hand, realizing after she spoke that she'd called him *tu*.

He pulled his hand away, she looked down, didn't want to watch him leave. The lawyer's words were coming back to her in salvos. She was to inherit all her father's property; he had left a letter for her, to which Paul had added the one he had read at the funeral. She lay down. An hour went by. Sayoko came to tell her that she was going out, that Paul would be there for dinner, that she must get some sleep. Rose remained silent. After a short while, her phone rang, she saw *Paul* light up the screen. She heard him say: Rose, don't worry, I'll be there tonight. Come back now, she murmured. He hung up. She begged the maple, invoked the mosses at the temple, their call, their light touch. She heard a noise, went to the hall, slid the front door open, and found herself face to face with Paul.

She laughed. He took a step forward and kissed her.

11

Murmurs have it that during the Ashikaga shogunate, Sesshū, the master of ink and wash painting, was the true inventor of abstract painting. He was a great prodigy of drawing and composition, but he liked nothing better than to splash a still-virgin scroll with random drops of ink. One day, a rich client, surprised by such fantasy, asked him what he expected from it. The branch of a cherry tree, answered the artist, and before the astonished nobleman's eyes, he transformed black fireflies into a branch spotted with petals. Painting is just improvisation, then? asked the nobleman. The world is like a cherry tree one has not looked at for three days, answered Sesshū.

THE WORLD IS LIKE A CHERRY TREE

He held her close to him as far as the room, looked in her eyes while they undressed; she felt as if she were seeing a man's body for the first time. When he entered her, she held him, desperately eager; he put his arms behind her back, and held her with equal force, burying his face in her neck. The sensual gratification was veiled by an unfamiliar, more powerful sensation—this is *intimacy*, she thought suddenly, and the intoxication of this discovery mingled with her pleasure. Later, he looked again into her eyes, and she felt tears running down her cheeks. He came with a cry of relief, of wrenching sorrow, of gratitude. The intensity of their intimacy overwhelmed her; other men had never fully inhabited their bodies for her; it intoxicated her to think that this body was Paul's. He lay on his back and wrapped his arms around her, but, after a moment, he pushed her gently to one side and gazed at her. They fell asleep to the sound of the rain. Before long, Rose awoke with a start. She was alone. She sat up, heard water running, fell back against the sheets. Paul came out of the bathroom, dressed, his hair wet. He crouched down next to her.

"Sayoko will be back soon," he said. "I'll take you out to dinner."

She studied his eyes; he pulled her up, held her close to him, and kissed her. She had a shower and got dressed, put on lipstick, went into the maple room.

"Sayoko will be here soon," he said.

In the hall, she paused by a tall, black earthenware vase, volcanic with branches of frothy white lilacs.

"Rose," he called.

They fled through the sodden garden. In the car, he put his hand on hers, gave brief instructions to Kanto, made a phone call. The end of the day was deepening into a twilit brilliance; a harsh, tapering light rose from the dark sky, fringing the clouds; the streets sped by like comets. Again the center, a dark passageway, an elevator to the top floor. They didn't speak, looked at each other. At the top, they came out into a room one side of which was entirely of glass, apparently frameless; the joint with the walls was invisible. The mountains to the East slept there like mute giants, as light poured down from unseen wellheads. To the right, in an alcove, a vase of clay was bursting with unfamiliar branches. They were led to a table by the picture window, and the sake arrived at once. Paul served them and leaned back in his chair. Between two intakes of breath, Rose waited.

"I'm sorry I ran away," he began.

She tried to speak, but he stopped her, raising his hand.

"I want to tell you what this week has been like for me."

He was smiling, she smiled back.

"I've known you for twenty years, but when you arrived, in spite of everything I knew about you, I was stunned. On the photographs, all that's visible is your indifference, your sadness. I was prepared to confront Haru's daughter, and, instead, there was a strange woman in front of me."

He took a sip of sake.

"I wasn't expecting any of who you are."

"And who am I?" she asked, thinking: I ask this question every day.

"I wonder."

Then, thoughtfully:

"A forceful flower, though, yes."

After a moment, he added:

"Although I owe it to the truth to point out that you weep every five minutes."

Sashimi was brought, he thanked the waitress, said a few words. She bowed respectfully, and Rose understood that he had asked for them not to be disturbed.

"When I saw you kneeling and touching the ground in the cemetery, I loved you with a strength beyond measure. So I ran away to Tōkyō. When Sayoko passed on your message, I took the first train, but I didn't know what to do. I was petrified."

Through the huge window, Rose could see the glow of mountains, their kindliness, motionless heroines. She felt as if she were becoming rooted in some unfamiliar substance and was afraid of being swept away, again, by the storm.

"How was Sayoko able to pass on my message if you were in Tōkyō?"

"She took a picture with her phone."

"She read it?"

"She doesn't speak French."

"You don't have to, to understand."

He looked at her, amused.

"Is peace of mind possible for people like us?" she asked. And as he did not reply, she added, "For people who have suffered as much as we have?"

He said nothing.

"Up to now, I've never managed to find it," she said.

"We've just spent a few days in a no-man's-land. Now real life is beginning. Who can tell what will happen? But I'm ready to try."

He stroked her hand.

"I'm eager to try," he said.

She leaned toward him; a tear rolled down her cheek.

"I cannot imagine leaving this place," she murmured.

In his gaze she saw, fleetingly, the same strange tenderness that, earlier, had made her believe there was another woman.

"Only Anna, from time to time, can make me forget the taste of misfortune," he said. "Tonight, it's not there. I thought the point was to survive, but maybe it's about dying and being reborn."

She thought of Keisuke Shibata, what remained of him, his emaciated soul.

She took a tuna sashimi, and the tender, oily flesh calmed her.

"I can't go back to Haru's with you," Paul said. "Sayoko will be spending the night there, and Anna is waiting for me. Tomorrow morning, I'm taking her to a play. I'll come and get you afterward."

Disappointed, disoriented, she put down her chopsticks.

"You have two letters to read," he added.

A woman came up to them, and Rose saw it was Beth Scott.

"Beth," said Paul, standing up and giving her a kiss on the cheek. "What brings you here?"

"A business dinner," she said, pointing to a group of Japanese men at a table near the entrance.

And to Rose:

"Would you like to have tea with me tomorrow morning?"

Rose, taken by surprise, nodded. The Englishwoman said something in Japanese to Paul, and he consented. She was about to leave, then turned around and added a few words. He looked astonished, gave a short answer. Rose followed her with her eyes as she went back to her table, made the men in suits laugh, and called the waitress, who came running and bowed deeply.

"What did she say?" asked Rose.

"The name of the place you'll meet tomorrow."

"And after that?"

He hesitated.

"*Yononaka wa mikka minu ma no sakura kana.* The world is like a cherry tree one has not looked at in three days. An old proverb."

She was thoughtful for a moment.

"What did you reply?"

He was silent.

"After ashes, roses," he said, finally.

He stood up, and she followed him to the door. He waved to Beth. In the elevator, he pulled her to him and kissed her. Outside, they were caught by rain and wind; he got into the car for a moment but left the door open.

"Who translated the letters?" she asked. "Was it you? Will I survive? Or will Sayoko have to wrap me up in a giant shawl?"

He smiled.

"I translated the letters," he said.

He leaned over to her, kissed her lightly on the lips, and left.

Back at the house, she went up to her room, got undressed, lay down in the dark, and was awake for a long time, until a nocturnal parting in the clouds revealed a silvered moon. She fell asleep in a sensation of grace. In the morning, she awoke with a start, got dressed quickly, went to the maple room, and found Sayoko at her low table.

"You meet Scott-san at eleven," she told her. "Kanto-san coming at ten forty-five."

Rose's phone rang. Paul's voice said: Rose. She laughed, responded: Paul. He laughed in turn. I'll see you this afternoon, he said. She hung up. She went back to her room, took her father's letters from the lawyer's file, returned to the main room, put them down on the floor by the glass cage. Sayoko peered at her over her glasses; Rose asked for a coffee and stretched out on the low sofa. At a quarter to eleven, she left the house. A pale sun broke through a pale mist, the morning fading into gray indifference. After a short ride, Rose got out at a modern building of light wood; along the large picture windows, there were sliding panels of the same light wood, their openwork like modern lace. All around ran a canal of black stone. Inside, a half-vault ceiling arched with slats of curved wood. Everything was transparency, spare and uncluttered, the motionless waters reflecting the splendor of the sky. On the other side, on a green lawn, was a garden with a maple, a cherry tree, dwarf bamboo, and an orange *torii*—I could live here, she thought. She spotted Beth at the back of the room. The décor was black and beige, sober. At the front, there were low bookshelves, and art books exhibited on lecterns. Rose glimpsed images in the open books of wooden galleries, tea plantations, kimonos. Beth looked up.

"You look terrific," she said.

Rose sat down across from her. The Englishwoman's phone rang. She listened, said a few words in Japanese, then hung up, saying, "Sayoko is watching over you."

"What was her relation to my father?" asked Rose.

"Her relation? She was his housekeeper for over forty years. He would have entrusted her with his life, in addition to his bookkeeping and his laundry."

"Does she have a husband? Children?"

"And grandchildren, like the majority of women like her, overwhelmed by duty, sacrifice, chores, and silence. Haru's death was a tragedy for Sayoko, but you'll never hear a word of complaint from her."

"She doesn't like you very much," said Rose.

"That's a euphemism," said Beth, "but, in a way, I understand. Japanese women are a light in a prison, and here I am, a free woman, trailing my melancholy through their temples and gardens."

Rose was brought a bowl of matcha set in the center of a black lacquered tray. On the white ceramic, the branch of a cherry tree in bloom expired a few millimeters from the upper edge.

"That's unusual at this time of year," said Beth. Her bowl was brown, furrowed, without decoration.

"Well then," she said, "you and Paul."

Rose said nothing.

"Life is full of wonder," said Beth. "I'd misjudged you; you're not incapable of changing."

"I can surprise you even more," said Rose. "Who's to say I won't throw myself in the river tomorrow."

Beth gave a short laugh.

"There are not many men I respect as much as I respect Paul," she said. "Do you deserve him? Clara was charming, she enchanted him, gave him a life that was light and luminous. You are rough, austere, absolute, you haven't charmed him, you've touched his heart. He was probably assuming that someday he'd find a peaceful life with another Clara, regain that sort of happiness, and suddenly you show up with your melancholy, your rage, and your bad temper."

She took a sip of tea and added:

"It won't be easy."

Rose ran her fingertips briefly over the edge of her bowl.

"You lost a son, didn't you?" she asked.

She knew that her words took Beth's breath away, she saw her blink, and admired her self-control.

"You've got intuition," Beth said, finally.

"You're hard and cold, but you look on Paul as a son," said Rose.

Beth's smile was joyless.

"And you're hard, too," she said, "but you're doing me good, because I can see that you find the same relief in this place as I do."

Rose was disconcerted.

"Anywhere else, I would find such beauty aggressive. Only

here does loss seem less cruel. Why? I'm not sure I really want to know, I'm afraid this respite might vanish into thin air. But when I walk through these gardens that are as sharp as stone, as soft as moss, I become another woman, someone who, for a brief moment, can accept what happened. You don't survive the death of a son; you're transformed into someone else who, from time to time, finds a way to breathe again."

She looked at Rose, her gaze sad and tired.

"I've liked you since we first met," she said, "and believe me, that doesn't happen often. You're about to stake your all, win or lose; don't ruin your chances."

"That's an interesting question," said Rose. "Can you lose what you haven't yet received?"

As she was saying *received*, she thought of Paul with such intense desire that she had to lower her eyes.

"The hardest thing is not being able to give anymore," Beth replied. "I was once a woman who loved, who would have walked through fire for the person I loved. I lost that, through my own fault, and since that day I've been more dead than alive."

She gave a laugh, full of weary irony, and elegantly drew her hand across her forehead. She pointed to Rose's bowl.

"The flower of the cherry tree has great power. That pretty air it shows off is a mask. With its spirit, its exuberance, it is all ruthless appetite and lust for life, the urge to try or die trying."

"But in the end it does die," said Rose.

"In the end we all die, yes," said Beth, "so we might as well let life improvise the music we play."

She squeezed Rose's hand affectionately.

"Otherwise," she said, "it's hell before hell."

She pulled her hand away and stood up.

"His name was William. He was twenty when he committed suicide. It was thirty years ago, it was yesterday."

Rose watched her walk away, upright and distinguished in

her unfathomable pain. Then she left the tea house, too, and asked Kanto to take her home.

In the deserted maple room, she went over to the letters lying on the floor, saw again the branch of the cherry tree dying just there by her lips, imagined the flowers, their petal exuberance—their appetite, voraciousness, their mad urge to try and to live. She broke the seal on an envelope, read the first words, and put the sheet of paper back down on the table. Rose, her father wrote, the world is like a cherry tree one has not looked at for three days.

12

In the chaotic times of the Japanese Middle Ages, which chroniclers of the era referred to as *an upside-down world*, there was a samurai and esthete, equally skilled in the arts of the saber and of calligraphy, who periodically returned to his home in Kagoshima on the island of Kyūshū. There he was reunited with his wife and son and, in the inner garden surrounded by wooden galleries, a magnificent maple tree. When the boy was old enough to express his desire to explore the archipelago, his father pointed to the tree with its flamboyant autumn leaves and said: Every mutation can be found within it, it is freer than I am; be the maple and travel within your transformations.

BE THE MAPLE

S he took the other letter and opened it. Paul had hand-written a short introduction: *I won't translate the open-ing formalities with the names, titles, and polite phrases; I'll begin with the statement itself.* She was moved by his broad, regular handwriting. Underneath, the text had been typed, then printed on thin paper. At the end, Haru had signed with his seal. He wrote: *At the gates of death, I find myself con-fronted with the imperious urge to tell you what I have kept from you for nearly my entire adult life. Forty years ago I fell in love with a Frenchwoman. From this ephemeral love, a daughter was born, who will soon come to Kyōto to hear my last will and testament. She did not know me, but she will know you. As your servant, who is forever indebted to you, I humbly ask you to pro-vide her with a warm welcome.* Rose's hand was trembling. Again she saw the cemetery, its shivering wooden stems, its lichen-covered stones, its stairways for ghosts; she imagined Paul at Haru's grave, a few steps from his wife's grave, a few steps from Nobu's; she pictured him, before that, reading this letter to a silent gathering. She put the sheet of paper down on the table and picked up the first letter again.

Rose, the world is like a cherry tree one has not looked at for three days. Yesterday, you were a joyful child, a wounded ado-lescent, an angry young woman, but the world turns so quickly that I am writing to a woman from the past when it is to the woman you are becoming that I would like to write. In the hour of one's death, it is remarkably easy to draw up the inventory of one's life. Everything has been sorted; all that remains are the bare bones of existence, reduced to the vital marrow. Nothing, I know now, has been stronger than your arrival in the world. Of the forty years that have since gone by, what matters most is that I have loved you. What sort of father would I have been if, after decades of absence, I had inflicted the burden of my illness upon you? What could I have given you that I cannot give you through my words? They spare you the sight of this wretched body, the terror of lost battles, love turned to punishment. Instead, I must share my admiration as a father and my joy that you have been in my life. I have watched you grow, fall down, get back up, still whole, still unique, still unhappy. Here in Japan, our tormented islands have taught us the implacability of misfortune. It is through these native tribulations that we have learned how to transform our land of cataclysms into a paradise; hence, the gardens of our temples are the soul of this country of disaster and sacrifice. Through our shared blood, you have come to know the beauty and tragedy of the world in a way in which the French, nourished by their more clement lands, cannot understand. In this upside-down era that is sold to us as modern, it's your Japanese soul that has the power to transform disenchantment and hell into a meadow of flowers. Don't be angry with me for having dragged you from one temple to the next; it has been a false prank and a true source of hope, because I know how these places can appease and transform. Aimless walking and words, more than property and works of art, constitute my true legacy. You are a forceful, unpredictable, opinionated flower; I have faith in your strength and your determination, and I remain hopeful, too, that these decades of silence will not have been in vain, that through this letter, despite my death, you will accept my heart, you will receive my love. And then, without trouble or tragedy, my entire life will pass into you.

Rose lay on the floor, arms outspread. The maple quivered gently. I'm at home, she thought, and she laughed. Long afterward, she heard the front door slide and Paul's steps approaching. He sat down next to her and propped himself on one arm as he passed the other over her waist. She realized she was weeping, silently, tears as fluid and regular as rain. He caressed her brow, collected a teardrop on his finger. She looked at him, he took her in his arms, and they went into the bedroom. She pulled him to her with the vigor of a drowning woman and embraced him as she had the day before. Will a day come, she wondered, when I will desire him in any other way? Between them there was a gravity that gave fervor to every gesture; to Rose their nakedness seemed like a miracle; the pleasure was violent, happy; Paul gazed at her like a man who has been relieved of a burden, with a virgin joy. In pleasure, his face was one she had never seen, cleansed of sorrow, luminous. She pressed herself against him, her back to his chest, he put his arms around her, placed his forehead on her nape. Later, they looked at each other. Paul groped behind him for his jacket and took out an envelope that bore Haru's seal.

"The original," he said.

She got to her knees, observed the two characters in the red ink of the seal.

"It is one of the most complex ideograms there is in Japanese," he added.

"It's not his name?" she asked, but at that very moment, she understood and murmured, "Rose."

"No one knew until he died."

She opened the envelope and took out two near-translucent sheets of paper. The lines with their black ink looked to her like wild grasses. On the upper left side, above the text, a few isolated characters had gone astray, and she touched them lightly with her fingertip.

"*Beyond, the dew alone reigns*," Paul translated.

Then, as she raised an eyebrow, questioning:

"It's the line by Keisuke that Haru had carved on his tombstone."

Again she saw the pearls of rain on the moss at Saihō-ji and thought she could make out the distorted reflection of a face.

"He grew up near a mountain torrent," she said. "I would have imagined, rather, a poem about icy water."

"Haru imagined life as a river to be crossed, with waters so deep they have become black. One day, I heard Keisuke say to him, 'You've got it right, the dew is on the far shore.'"

She sensed an unfamiliar whispering within and looked again at the text of moving grasses.

"It's beautiful writing," she said.

"Haru was a merchant, a samurai, but above all an esthete."

"A true Japanese," she remarked.

"Not for everything," he said. "In some respects, he was atypical, he didn't share the tastes of Japanese men of his generation. He had no intention of getting married or founding a family; he didn't patronize geishas, let alone hostesses. There were quite a few Western women in his life."

"Was Beth one of them?"

"Yes."

"She loved Japanese men?"

"She loved all men. She had many lovers, even when she was married."

"I've had a lot of lovers, too," said Rose.

"So I saw," he said with a smile. "But you weren't married."

"I don't remember any of them," she murmured.

He fell silent.

"Why didn't Haru leave you anything?" she asked.

"I refused."

He sat up, grimaced.

"We'll talk about it later," he said. "Sayoko will be coming, and I want to take you somewhere."

"Why do you limp?" she asked.

He didn't answer, went to the bathroom, and came out showered and dressed. She was struck by how relaxed his features seemed, by the light in his gaze; she got up and went over to him; he held her in his arms, kissed her, laughed with the lightheartedness of a child. She had her shower and got dressed in turn, and went to join him in the maple room, seized by a sudden reverence. The tree rose toward clouds of ash, its branches spread like wings, its leaves trembling, reaching out to the great invisible blaze. What is happening? she wondered. She looked at the sky with its gray clouds, heavy with turbulence and storm, and the maple grew even taller.

"Rose?" Paul called, from the hallway.

She tore herself from her contemplation of the tree in flight, began to walk away, then turned back one last time and, on impulse, bowed. In the entrance, Paul held an umbrella out to her, but just as she was walking toward him, she saw the frothy flocks of white lilac, stopped again, tried to arrest a fleeting thought. She went closer to the disheveled clusters on the tender wealth of foliage and felt the thought fade. She followed Paul; in the car, she took his hand and lifted it to her lips. They were speeding eastward. Kanto stopped by a wide lane of pine trees and azalea shrubs that rose toward the hill. The avenue led to a high carved wooden gate with a thatched roof, then continued to climb. It was drizzling, they walked slowly.

"Two years after Clara's death, Keisuke and I jumped into the river," he said. "We were completely drunk. We climbed over the railing of the Sanjo bridge, I landed on a rock, he landed no problem. Afterward, at the hospital, he said: Hell is when even death doesn't want you. But hell, to me, was that I had failed Anna."

"What did you tell her?"

"The truth. That her father was an idiot who had drunk too much."

He laughed.

"She was four years old. She said, 'Then drink just a little.'"

The lane narrowed; finally, it reached a stone wall; through a metal gate, they could see tiers of tombs.

"It was hard to translate Haru's letter," he said. "His decision, before, was difficult. I wish you had known him."

He stopped at the metal gate.

"Where are we?" she asked.

"Higashi Ōtani."

"Who is here?"

"No one I know. But it's an important gathering place for the celebration of Obon, the feast of the dead."

They entered the cemetery perched on the hillside with dozens of rows of closely aligned graves, a mad tide of mute gray stone. The cries of crows rent the silence; she liked their strange, croaking call. Paul took the path toward the upper levels, she followed him along stairways that changed directions, arrived behind him, breathless, at the top row. He was leaning against a railing; she joined him, took in the view. At their feet, the gigantic mausoleum; beyond, the panorama of the sky, and Kyōto, the city of wonders; in the distance, the dark summits of Arashiyama unfolding against the twilight. It had stopped raining, the sky was ghostly, ashen, edged with black streaks that fringed the clouds.

"And Obon?" she asked.

"During Obon, the spirits of the ancestors are honored; they are thanked for their sacrifices, people visit their family tombs, sometimes far from home, offerings are made to the dead to relieve their troubles. The festivities last a month, but for the grand finale ten thousand lanterns are lit, here, at Higashi Ōtani."

"Offerings to relieve the dead of what sort of troubles?"

"It is said that *Obon* derived from a sūtra in Sanskrit that means 'hanging upside down in hell.'"

In this upside-down era, she thought, then: Everything has been upside-down in my life—I know my father through the child he once was and through the man I desire. Paul was looking at her, she went closer to him, he put his arm around her. Below them, Kyōto was disappearing in the night. All around, the graves, dusted with a dew from a far shore, quivered with the invisible life of the dead. Paul kissed her on her temple.

"We're survivors," he said, "until others survive us."

And so, there in the great necropolis of souls hanging upside down, Rose became someone else. In a flash, she saw the maple again, in its glass cage: rooted in the fluidity of the moss yet free under the sky, giving life all around it in its countless mutations, it whispered music to her, of foliage and breezes; she let herself drift on it without fear, without anger; at the edges of her perception glided her father's gardens and a few branches of white lilac, a dissolving farandole of trees and flowers. She breathed in, smelled the perfume of earth and stone, of the end of things. She realized that Paul was weeping, without sadness, surrendering to his tears, to her presence, to his desire for her. She let out a silent cry within, a terrible, magnificent cry, which brought her birth and death—and rebirth, at last.

"There is only love," said Paul. "Love and, then, death."

ACKNOWLEDGMENTS

Thanks and gratitude to Jean-Marie
Laclavetine, Pierre Gestède, Jean-Baptiste
Del Amo, Elena Ramírez Rico.